UNFAITHFUL

Once Broken   Some Hearts

Can't Be Mended

A Novel

Billie Dureyea Shell

Published by:
L.O. Quent Publishing House
Los Angeles, CA
Email: athenawhite111078@yahoo.com

Cover Design : Kevin Allen
Second Printing : November 2013
ISBN: 978-0-615-87904-8
1098765432

To my brother, the late Zain Lamar Addison

I miss you so much. We love you.

ACKNOWLEDGMENTS

First and foremost, I give all praise to my Lord and Savior Jesus Christ who not only died on the cross for my sins, but who also loves me, "ME" unconditionally and without merit. Thank you Lord for all the wonderful blessing you've giving me including my gift of writing. I worship you and praise your Holy name. Without you, none of this would have been possible. I love you and thanks for loving and forgiving me!

To my beautiful and loving wife, Athena. I thank you and love you so much. You are my sunshine and my shining star. You loved me when I was on and off, on top and at the bottom. We've been to hell and back together. I couldn't have made it through the journey without you by my side. You and only you have the key to my heart with yo stank'n ass ☺ ! I love you pooh, you're my heart1436.

To my children; Jazmine, Ant'Juan, Anthony, Lil Dureyea, my princess Alura and my little man Cameron. There is no

To my brother, the late Zain Lamar Addison

I miss you so much. We love you.

ACKNOWLEDGMENTS

First and foremost, I give all praise to my Lord and Savior Jesus Christ who not only died on the cross for my sins, but who also loves me, "ME" unconditionally and without merit. Thank you Lord for all the wonderful blessing you've giving me including my gift of writing. I worship you and praise your Holy name. Without you, none of this would have been possible. I love you and thanks for loving and forgiving me!

To my beautiful and loving wife, Athena. I thank you and love you so much. You are my sunshine and my shining star. You loved me when I was on and off, on top and at the bottom. We've been to hell and back together. I couldn't have made it through the journey without you by my side. You and only you have the key to my heart with yo stank'n ass ☺ ! I love you pooh, you're my heart1436.

To my children; Jazmine, Ant'Juan, Anthony, Lil Dureyea, my princess Alura and my little man Cameron. There is no words that could ever express how much I love you. I'll die for you in a heartbeat. My heart is made for Athena and it beats for all of you. Daddy will always have ya'll back no matter what you do…promise!

To my mom, Mc'Lessie Shell what can I say? Without you there would be no me. I love you and I'll always be there when you need me. Thank you for bringing me into the world and doing all you could to raise me right. You did a damn fine job.

To my grandson, Lil Dude. Grandpa got you fo sho! I'm gonna spoil you past rotten ☺! April, thanks for always being a friend, I'm glad you found you a cool dude and tell him I said, "What's up?"

Zanna and Zalen, ya'll are my first cousins and also my Brother Zane's kids. I love ya'll like my own. Zanna, Uncle is here and I don't give a damn what.

It is I, got you I'm proud of you and I love you. Tora, You know I love yo ass, thanks for holding my nigga Zanc down. You know no matter where I'm at, you call me and I'm there. I love you cousin. Cousin Ty, Nigga what it do. Nigga, you know I got you and I know you got me. I love you big cousin and I miss you. Thanks for always being real with me and Zane. Auntie Chris, You are the reason I've always believed in myself from birth. I've been yo "man." Thanks for always believing in me. I love you. Uncle Cal, I love you, you know that. Uncle Woody,

I know how to be a man because I didn't have a dad around, you was the closest I had to one. I love you, Unc. Jamal, Me, you and Scar trouble from the start. I love you Bro, no matter what. Nigga, I got you!

Juggie, Bro, you a real nigga, don't change. I love and miss you. To all you mutha fucka's who never had my back and I had yours, man fuck you with a broomstick. If I didn't bring you up, it's because you don't mean shit to me. If you were dying of thirst, I wouldn't piss in your mouth. Fuck you! Ooh Barbara Neal, "Ma," I love you. Casta Sis, I love you. Salena, My favorite niece, I love you. Samaja, Love you. Lil Brain, Nigga love you. Punken, Love yo ass nigga. Lil Bro Anthony, Love you, it might be a few, I forgot. Peanut, Love you. Nieces and nephews, Uncle love ya'll. To Lynnnette's family, I'm sorry for ya'll lost. She was a good person. Denise, I love you. Glenda, I love you. I will always love you, Lil Sis (Blackie). To the readers, Enjoy, I am a real nigga, love it or hate it, let me know! Dureyea.

PROLOGUE

I CAN'T BELIEVE THIS NIGGA IS doing me like this, Nicole thought to herself, as she sat across the street from her and Billie's house in the neighbor's driveway in a rented Dodge Charger. She could see their front door clearly, as if she was sitting in front of the house itself. She checked her Movado watch for the third time. It was 3:07 a.m. The watch was a gift from Billie on her twenty-sixth birthday.

A tear fell from her eye, as she remembered the party he threw for her and how after the party was over, he took her to Santa Monica Beach, laid a blanket on the sand, placed rose pedals all over it, then made love to her while the sun came up. That was the first time Nicole had ever seen a sunrise.

"Fuck this black motherfucker!" she yelled out, as she wiped the tears from her eyes with the back of her hand. She grabbed her Coach purse, checking for the 40 Cal Roger she had placed inside it before going to Hertz Rent-A-Car at LAX Airport earlier. *If this motherfucker tries to play me today, I'ma give it to his ass*, she said to herself, as she ran her hand across and over the smooth black steel. *But if he keeps it real, we can work through this as a family. The choice will be his!*

Nicole closed her purse, and sat it on her lap. He will decide his own fate. Rubbing her stomach, she felt Billie's child growing inside her. *Please God, for the sake of our baby, let him keep it real with me!*

Nicole noticed Billie's car turning the corner. She ducked her head, just as he was pulling into their driveway. Billie hopped out his car with his Galaxy III, and headed for the front door, laughing at whoever was on the other end. Nicole sucked her teeth. "Probably some chicken head bitch!" she said, rubbing her stomach again. "I hope your Daddy loves me as much as he claims, because I'm done playing games with him!" Nicole hopped out the Dodger Charger, holding tightly to the 40 Cal and her purse. She shut the door softly, so that he wouldn't hear it, and ran across the street. She jogged the few feet that separated her from their home. As Billie was putting the key in the door, Nicole raised the gun, pointing it at his back. Billie was so wrapped up in his phone conversation he didn't even notice Nicole creeping up on him.

"Man, a nigga can't wait to see you either. Shit, and if you puttin' it down on me like you did last time, I'ma say fuck packing an overnight bag, we can—"

Click Clock was the sound Billie heard, as he opened the door, which cut his conversation short.

"If who doing it like what, motherfucker?" Nicole asked though clenched teeth, holding the gun a few feet away from his back.

Billie tried to turn around to face his would-be jacker.

"Naw, nigga, stay facing forward!" Nicole ordered. "See what happens when you cupcaking? Now go on and step in the house, we need to talk. Oh, and reach me yo' goddamn phone! And for your own sake, don't try to be a hero and spin around on me, 'cause I will put a slug in yo' ass!"

"Cola?" Billie asked, as he reached his phone back, recognizing her voice. Cola was a name he had given her in middle school because her body was shaped like an old school Coca-Cola bottle.

Nicole snatched the phone out of his hand, and placed it to her ear. Sure enough, just as she had thought, it was a chicken head bitch. "Look, bitch, Billie gotta go. He got some business to handle at home right now, and when he's done, I'm pretty sure, as a matter of fact, I'm one hundred percent positive you'll be the last person he will want to talk to, so deuces! Ooh, yeah, and don't call this phone anymore!"

"Who the fuck is this?" the now angry black woman, who was on Billie's phone, yelled.

"Bitch, I'm Nicole. I'm Billie's bitch and like I said, lose this motherfuckin' number."

Nicole slammed Billie's phone on the porch, breaking it into several pieces.

"Ay, Cola, what the fuck? I just got that phone," Billie said, trying to look over his shoulder when he heard his phone being destroyed.

"Fuck that phone," Nicole yelled, shoving him in the house. The push caught Billie off guard, making him trip over the welcome mat. He fell to the floor face first. She slammed the door behind them!

"Ay, Cola, you on some bullshit," he said through clenched teeth, mad as a bull. He couldn't believe he had gotten caught slipping. And, what made it even worse, his girl caught him. Billie slowly turned around to face her, and tried to get up off the floor.

"Naw, nigga, stay yo cheating ass down there, motherfucker," Nicole said, taking four steps so that she was standing directly over him; gun pointed at his head. "And for the record, it's you that's on and has been on some bullshit. Now listen, Billie, or do you prefer, Playa Playa?" She went on without letting him answer. "I love you with all my heart and soul. I will do anything for you; if necessary, I'll put my life on the line for you." Nicole looked him in his eyes as she spoke, tears running down her face.

"I know this, Cola," Billie replied, confusion written all over his face.

"Okay, well, since you claim you know, I'm only going to give you one chance, Billie, just one chance to tell me the truth. If you know how much I love you and you claim you love me the same, then that's all you need. But first, I want you to know that I'm pregnant. I found out three days ago. I'm going to have our baby, Billie," Nicole said, with a smirk on her face. "The doctor told us that I couldn't have kids, but God is good and He has blessed us to have one. The Lord has answered my prayers!"

"You're pregnant?" Billie's mouth was wide open in disbelief. "But I thought—"

Nicole cut him off. "Billie, I'm fuckin' pregnant…okay? Fuck what you thought. Now back to the issue at hand. I hope this new information I just gave you about you being a, Daddy helps you to be truthful with me, but like I said, you only get one chance to tell me the truth. Don't play with me, Billie. I want a straight answer from you. Are you fucking Tasha and is that your little bastard child she's carrying?"

Billie broke eye contact with Nicole and looked away. "Um, Nicole, I…I…"

Nicole squeezed the trigger, firing off a round into this leg.

"*Aaahhhh, shit,*" Billie cried out.

"Nigga, don't 'I…I' me. Are you fucking her?" Nicole asked in an even tone.

"Ohhh, God, this shit hurts. Bitch, you done lost your mind. I'ma fuck you—"

Nicole squeezed the trigger, again, firing two shots—one into the floor between his legs, the other in his left thigh.

"Oh, Lord, help me!" Billie screamed out in pain.

"Play time is over, nigga. Now answer my damn question!" Nicole said, with a look in her eyes that told Billie she was not going to hesitate pulling the trigger again.

"Okay, okay, Cola! Ooh God. Yeah, I fucked her, but it didn't mean shit. I love you—"

Nicole laughed out loud. "Fuck all that love shit, 'cause if you loved me you would have kept yo dick in yo pants!" She spoke with conviction. "Now, is it your baby she's carrying?" Nicole asked, looking him in his eyes.

"Ummmmm, what, baby? I don't know about no—"

Nicole fired three shots into the floor next to Billie's head. He balled up in a fetal position.

Nicole took out her phone and dialed 911. "My name is Nicole White and my fiancée has just been shot by someone who broke into our home. Can you please send help? Please!" Her voice cracked as she spoke.

"Yes, Ma'am, are you hurt?" the operator asked.

"No, I'm fine, but he is shot. Please send help!"

"Okay, Ma'am, help is on the way. Can you please—"

Nicole hung up the phone, cutting the operator's off as she wiped her face. Nicole pointed the gun at Billie's head.

"Now, I have one more question for you?" Nicole said, with a frown on her face. Billie looked up, tears now running from his eyes. "Are you going to make her have an abortion or do you want her to keep it?"

"Cola, I...I—"

She pulled the trigger again, firing off three rounds!

CHAPTER 1

Three months earlier…

"DAMN, BITCH, YOU GOT A FLY ass house," Tasha said, as she entered Nicole's and Billie's new home in Ladera Heights. "Y'all motherfuckers doing the most," Tasha stated as she walked through their newly furnished living room. A 92" Sony LCD HD TV hung on the wall with the base surround sound system playing YG's newest CD while the TV displayed the video. The picture was so clear it seemed like YG was standing in the living room in person. As Tasha entered the kitchen, she noticed what was on the other side of the double, sliding glass doors.

"Oohh, hell naw, bitch, it's on! We gotta have a pool party at this motherfucker!"

Nicole laughed while she got herself a Sprite out the refrigerator. "Girl, do you want something to drink?" She asked thinking to herself how much she was not just her best friend, but was also like her sister.

"Naw, I'm good. Damn, bitch, you got a Jacuzzi, too?" Tasha asked in amazement.

"Yeah," Nicole answered with a smirk on her face, "and they're both heated."

Tasha gave Nicole a devilish grin. "Well, bitch, why we still standing here talking when we could be kicking back relaxing?"

Nicole sat her drink down and unlocked the glass doors. "Bitch, you ain't said nothin' but a word!"

They laughed, as they stepped outside and began removing their clothes. They had the bodies of goddesses. Standing five-foot-seven, Nicole weighed one thirty-seven pounds, with 36B breasts, a twenty-four-inch waist and her hips and ass were thirty-seven inches. She was shaped like an old school Coca-Cola bottle and that's how she got the nickname Cola! Her flawless honey-colored skin was the envy of many women with jet-black hair and light brown eyes. She made many men want to trick off their life savings and, to top it off, her ass was shaped like a heart. It was firm, but soft. Nikki Minaj didn't have shit on Nicole.

Tasha was a little shorter than her best friend was, but made up for it in all departments. Tasha was five-foot-five and one hundred thirty pounds of sheer beauty. She had long, baby hair that hung past her shoulders. Her skin was almond-colored and she had the most beautiful breath-taking hazel eyes. Tasha was a complete brick house, with 34C breasts, a twenty-four-inch waist and thirty-six inches of ass and hips. Tasha was the reason Nelly invented Apple Bottom jeans. Tasha was a thicker version of Stacy Dash and had been mistaken for her a thousand times. Many well-known rappers had approached Nicole and Tasha, trying to get them in their videos. Plies had done everything but get on his knees, trying to get them to be in his "Becky" video. They, however, always declined because they felt shaking their asses for cash was degrading. Plus, it only paid a few hundred dollars a video. They had good jobs, making over $28.00 an hour and from growing up in the hood, they knew niggas lost respect for you real quick if you were just another groupie bitch. Most of the video chicks did whoever and whatever for the whole crew after the video was over, just to be called for the next video and considered down.

After they stepped out of their clothes, Nicole hit the switch for the pool heater. They unhooked their bras and dove in the pool.

"Bitch, this is living," Tasha said after she came up for air and splashed water in Nicole's face.

Nicole splashed her back, giggling.

"You need to tell me your secret on how you fucking and sucking Billie's dick, so I can whip it on the next nigga I'm in a relationship with because I want a house like this.

Nicole started laughing, as she floated on her back. "Tee, yo ass is crazy, and you know it's more than my head and pussy that got him sprung. I been having his ass whipped since what, the seventh grade? That nigga walk, sleep and eat me!"

Tasha sucked her teeth. "Yeah, whatever, bitch! Yo ass dope, voodoo that nigga." Tasha tolled her eyes, as she thought back to herself on how in middle school Billie would always ask about Nicole when they were in class together.

"Shit, bitch, I remember when you used to be running from him. It was me who was telling you he was a cool nigga. Now yo ass be running behind him!"

"Fuck you, bitch!" Nicole laughed, as she splashed water in Tasha's face.

"Bitch, you know it's true," Tasha stated, trying to dodge the water while splashing Nicole back.

"Alright, Tee, I'll give you that, you on point. I do love my nigga, but he deserves my love, plus, bitch, the dick is awesome!"

Tasha's heart skipped a beat, hearing Nicole talk about Billie's sex game.

Since middle school, Tasha had been feeling Billie, but he was so gone and trapped up in Nicole that she never acted on her feelings. She had wanted to fuck Billie since the ninth grade.

"Yeah whatever, bitch," Tasha said, feeling her pussy throb at the thought of Billie fucking her. "Anyway, what's up for the weekend?" Tasha asked, changing the subject, but still thinking about how good Billie would feel between her thighs.

"Shit, I don't know yet. I'm hoping Billie come through on those tickets for the Trey Songz concert at the Forum on Sunday. If he do, you know we gotta go shopping on Saturday so we can be on point when we step in that motherfucker!"

Tasha put her hand together, as if she was praying. "Oooh Lord, please let him get those tickets 'cause you know I love me some Trey fine ass Songz!"

"Well, you don't have to hope nor pray anymore because I got em!" said Billie.

Nicole and Tasha turned around to see Billie standing in the doorway of the glass doors.

"Hey Daddy!" Nicole greeted. "How long you been standing there ear hustling?" She smiled from ear to ear.

Billie chuckled. "I wasn't ear hustling, boo, just overheard y'all talking as I was walking up. Plus, as loud as you two are, who in the world would have to ear hustle? I'm willing to bet a hundred dollars that the whole block now know y'all love Trey Songz."

Nicole and Tasha flipped him the bird, simultaneously saying, "Fuck you, we ain't that loud," Nicole declared, pouting and ghetto Tasha said, sucking her teeth.

"Yeah, okay," Billie said, sarcastically. "It's y'all's story. Tell it how you want to," he stated with a devilish grin. "I'm glad to see you both are enjoying the pool!" he said, noticing their bras by the pool and their clothes by the door.

Nicole stepped out the pool. The sight of her perfect breasts made him speechless. Before he could regain his senses, she had run over to him, giving him a hug and kiss.

"Umm hmmm, we sure are," Nicole whispered in his ear, then gave him another kiss. "I've missed you!"

"Girl, you getting a nigga all wet and shit, come on Cola, you know I am about my clothes!"

Nicole sucked her teeth, laughed, and stole another kiss before letting him go. "Fuck yo clothes." Nicole turned to run and got smacked on her ass.

Tasha laughed as Nicole dove back into the pool. "Y'all so stupid," she said, while splashing water toward Billie, defending her girl.

Billie closed the glass doors to keep from getting wet. Once Nicole came up from under the water, she joined Tasha in splashing water toward Billie. "Fuck yo clothes," Nicole yelled, still splashing water.

Billie laughed from behind the safety of closed doors. "Oh y'all got jokes. Fuck both of y'all," he stated, as he cut the heater off in the pool. He quickly opened the door, grabbed their clothes and shut the door before getting wet. Nicole and Tasha were so focused on splashing water his way that neither of them noticed what he had done.

"Oh y'all done fucked up," he yelled from behind the glass doors, holding up their clothes.

Nicole and Tasha hopped out of the pool, running toward the glass doors, giving Billie more than an eye full as their breasts bounced up and down with each step they took. Neither of them thinking nor concerned about their bras.

Damn, Billie said to himself, as they reached the doors and he locked them. His dick was hard as steel, as he looked at their now hardened nipples pointing directly at him.

"Okay, okay…no, please," Nicole said, as she tried the door.

"We're sorry," they yelled in unison, not wanting to be stuck outside without any clothes.

Nicole looked over at Tasha, laughing. Her laughing stopped as she realized that Tasha didn't have on a bra and was out the pool giving her man a full view of her full, firm breasts. Nicole quickly turned Tasha, facing her toward the pool. "Girl, yo bra!"

"Ohhh shit, bitch, my bad!" Tasha said, just realizing it herself.

Nicole giggled. "Bitch, don't trip. It was a spur of the moment thing. Neither one of us was thinking straight; all we wanted was our clothes."

Billie started laughing, as he took in the backside view of two of the baddest bitches in California. "What you bitches plotting?" he asked, as Nicole turned back around.

Tasha walked to the end of the pool, grabbed both their bras, put hers on then walked back to the glass doors handing Nicole hers.

"It's not like that, Daddy," Nicole said, looking into Billie's eyes with a smirk on her face. "You win. Can we please have our clothes back? We're sorry!"

Billie smiled. "Ooh I do?"

"Yeah, Daddy, you win. So can you open the doors and give us our clothes back, please?"

Nicole and Tasha was doing all they could to keep from laughing.

"Okay, I can give you both your clothes back, but under one condition."

Nicole knew it was too good to be true. "What's the condition?" she asked, not knowing what to expect.

"That both you bitches get y'all asses in here and cook me, the winner, some dinner!"

Nicole started laughing. Tasha rolled her eyes, giving him the middle finger.

"Nigga, fuck you and them clothes!" She joined Nicole in laughter.

"Yeah, fuck them clothes," Nicole agreed, then gave Tasha high-five.

"All right then have it y'all way. I'll just find me two other young, beautiful, grateful black women that want to see Trey Songz and don't mind feeding a nigga that had to pull some strings to get front row seats and back stage passes."

Billie dropped their clothes on the floor by the door and started walking away.

"Nigga, you better stop playing with me," Nicole said, trying not to smile.

Billie pulled out his cell phone. "Hmmm, let's see who I can call. Ooh yeah, Kelly from the gym!"

"Nigga, don't make me break this motherfuckin' glass door," Nicole said, with her hands on her hips.

Billie looked over his shoulder, smiling as he pulled the tickets out his pocket. "I could just rip them up. I don't care for Trey Songz anyway."

Nicole put her bra on and rolled her eyes.

Tasha looked at Nicole, feeling defeated. She took a deep breath, exhaled and then sucked her teeth. "I'll submit, Cola, if you will!"

Nicole sighed. "All right, all right, you got this round. We will cook for you!"

Billie walked back to the glass doors, placing the tickets back in his pocket. "Y'all give me your word!"

"We promise," they said in unison, together rolling their eyes.

Billie laughed, unlocked the doors, and took off running, as they slid them open. "I thought you bitches would see it my way."

While standing in the doorway that separated the kitchen from the living room, Nicole and Tasha mean mugged him while putting on their clothes, still by the glass doors, but now inside the kitchen.

"We gonna get yo ass back," Tasha stated while putting her shirt on.

"Whatever," Billie said, not entertaining her threat. "Oh yeah, just so y'all know, I want mac & cheese, greens, fried chicken and cornbread for my meal. Now chop chop!"

Nicole and Tasha picked up their shoes and threw them at Billie. He dodged them, laughing, as he ran up the stairs, yelling, "Chop chop!"

"Oohhhhhhh, he gets on my nerves," Tasha said, as they laughed. "That nigga always gets the best of us," Tasha said, while going to retrieve their shoes.

"Yeah, but we'll get him back, fo' sho. Now let's wash up so we can cook this nigga's food. You know I have some clothes that can fit you. Go on upstairs and pick out something, take you a shower and while you're doing that, I'll pull the chicken out the freezer, put the water on for the mac & cheese and start washing the greens. By the time you get back down here, the chicken will be seasoned, ready to be fried, the greens will be cleaned and the mac & cheese will be done. You can finish whatever I didn't while I go shower and get dressed."

"Shit, Billie probably up there finna play that damn P53 Black Ooze game he so in love with."

"Girl, we will both have showered, cooked the food and have it at the table before he even realize we've done anything at all. Go on upstairs; our room is on the left, right after you come off the stairs. Trust me; Billie is in his game room, well his man cave so he calls it. It's off limits to women!"

They laughed.

"Girl, you know how men need their toys and games," Tasha said, as she began walking toward the stairs. Tasha could hear shooting bombs going off and helicopters, as she started up the stairs.

Nicole got to work in the kitchen, shaking her head in agreement to Tasha's statement, as she placed the greens in the sink to be cleaned.

CHAPTER 2

TASHA FOUND A SUNDRESS THAT SHE liked, and then went through the closet looking for the shoes to match. Once she found them, she headed for the bathroom to shower. *Damn, this motherfuckin' bathroom is huge*, she stated to herself, as she began taking off her clothes, still looking around. It had marble floors, a shower the size of her whole bathroom with built-in seats and a sink. There was a Jacuzzi tub, his and her sinks, with granite countertops, a regular toilet and a bidet.

They ass is on, she thought to herself, as she stepped into the shower. Tasha could hear the fun fire and Billie yelling commands from the game room/man cave, as she closed the shower door. *Damn, he got that shit loud*, she said to herself, as she cut the water on.

As Tasha was showering, she noticed that there were eight other nozzles connected to the one she was using. Tasha tried them all. She giggled to herself, feeling the tickling sensation that one of the nozzles made her feel, as the water came out in little beads running over her body. Tasha noticed that there was even one with a vibrator. The thought crossed her mind to see how it would feel against here clit, as she cut it on hearing the low humming sound it made and loving the sensation it was sending through her hand by just holding it. Remembering how loud she got when having an orgasm, she quickly turned it off then stepped out of the shower. Tasha looked over her shoulder at the vibrating shower nozzle. *A bitch could get in trouble fucking with you.* She laughed out loud, while closing the shower and grabbing a terrycloth towel off the rack.

Tasha wrapped herself in the towel, and walked over to the sink. She bent down, opening the cabinet, hoping to find some lotion and hit the jackpot. She grabbed one of Nicole's Cucumber Melon Bath & Body Works spray and lotion sets and then walked to the toilet to sit down. She dropped her towel and began putting lotion on her beautiful, evenly toned skin. After she was done, Tasha sprayed herself lightly with the body spray, put on her bra, threw on the dress, without any panties, since they were still a little wet from her dive in the pool and replaced the lotion and body spray in the cabinet. Tasha slipped her feet into the shoes that matched the dress, and gave herself the once over in the mirror.

Tasha was about to exit the bathroom when she heard

someone entering the master bedroom that was adjoined to the bathroom she was in. Tasha stopped in her tracks and stood behind the door. Tasha heard someone going through the closet so she cracked the door to peek. Billie exited the closet with a pair of sweatpants and a white t-shirt. *Oh, it's on. I'm about to scare the living shit out this nigga*, Tasha stated to herself. Smiling from ear to ear, she was getting her chance at revenge from what he had done to her and Nicole earlier.

Just as Tasha was about to jump out to scare Billie, he pulled down his pants. Tasha saw his dick hanging out the front of his boxers and she froze. Her eyes were still glued to Billie's dick.

"Ooh my goodness," she moaned, then licked her lips. Catching herself, she pushed the door, closing it a little more so she wouldn't be seen, but leaving it open enough so she could still see out.

Billie adjusted his boxers so that his dick was back where it belonged. Tasha could still see the imprint.

"Damn, that nigga got a big ass dick," she said, under her breath, feeling her pussy getting wet.

Tasha continued to watch him as he put on the sweats and T-shirt and exited the room. Tasha stood by the bathroom door stuck for a minute, thinking about what she had seen. *Nicole ain't lying*, she thought to herself as she opened the door, exited the bathroom, walked through the master bedroom, still thinking about what she'd seen. She steps out into the hallway at the stairs right outside Nicole's bedroom.

Tasha looked down the hall. The video game was on blast. She thought about going in Billie's game room, pulling down his sweats and deep throating his dick 'til he came in her mouth. Her pussy throbbed as she played the image in her mind. Tasha let out a moan of pleasure at the thought of sucking Billie's dick. Hearing a bomb loudly go off in the game room snapped her out of her fantasy. "You're lucky you my girl," Tasha said out loud, thinking of Nicole, as she descended the stairs. "I swear yo ass is lucky…"

Tasha walked into the kitchen noticing that Nicole had already made the mac & cheese, cleaned the greens, seasoned the chicken and was about to start on the cornbread.

"Damn, Betty Crocker," Tasha said, making Nicole turn around as she mixed the eggs, milk, sugar and butter. "Bitch, yo, Daddy must have been an Octopus. I know I seen yo ass in *Men In Black III!*"

They started laughing.

"Naw, bitch, I just got that shit done, but since you tryin' to clown, I thought I was going to have to call the Coast Guard, you was up there so long. I started thinking you had drowned yo'self or got lost at sea. Where's Wilson at, bitch?" Nicole asked, giggling.

"My name ain't Tom Hanks, but for real a shark...shit, a killer whale could fit in that bathroom."

Nicole nodded her head in agreement. "I know, girl, that bathroom is so huge I'm thinking about putting a pool in it!"

They shared another laugh.

"Look, now that yo ass done finally came downstairs, I'm going to go clean myself up. All you gotta do is put the greens on the stove, stick the chicken in the fryer and finish mixing the cornbread, put it in a pan and then place it in the oven. I'll be back in like thirty minutes. You know my home is your home, etc., etc., so do you, bitch!"

Nicole took off her apron and put it on Tasha's neck then took off toward the stairs. "Ohh and by the way," Nicole said, looking around the door with one foot on the step, "You look good in that dress!"

Tasha rolled her eyes and snapped her fingers at the same time. "Bitch, I look good in anything I put on," Tasha responded then placed her hand on her hips, smiling. "So if you don't know, now you know!"

They broke out into laughter.

"Yeah, okay Biggie," Nicole said, as she went up the stairs to take her shower.

CHAPTER 3

NICOLE MADE IT TO THE TOP of the stairs. She was about to go into the master bedroom when she heard Billie yelling.

"Fuckin' get down, De'Shawn, you gonna get yo'self shot, you stupid motherfucker!"

Nicole giggled to herself, and then decided to peek in on him. Nicole loved watching him play his PS3, because he looked like a little kid while doing so. However, she did not like how he would sit up all damn night playing it, having her waiting till three or four clock in the morning sometimes for him to come to bed. On many nights, Nicole wanted some dick, but Billie was on one with that damn game. Nicole would try her best to wait up for him, but always wound up falling asleep, in which it seemed Billie always crawled his ass into bed seconds later. *One of these day's he is gonna make me break that motherfuckin' game system*, Nicole thought to herself, as she peeked around the door, hating Sony, all the people that worked for them and whomever invented the game Black Ops II.

Billie was sitting on his game chair with his controller in his and headset hanging off his ear, barking commands. Nicole looked at the fifty-two-inch TV noticing names over some of the men's heads that were on the screen—Zane, De'Shawn, Anthony and Jamal. She giggled to herself, realizing he was playing with his boys who recalled how happy Billie was when he explained to her that he and his boys could all play the game together from their own homes, but it would be as if they all were all in the same room.

My big baby, Nicole thought to herself as she entered the room and sat next to him. "Hey, Daddy, what's up?"

"What's up, babe, the food ready?" he asked, never taking his eyes off the screen.

"Almost," Nicole replied, and then began rubbing his leg.

"Damn, Zane, cover me," Billie yelled into the headset. Just as he completed the sentence, a man on a rooftop got shot in the head and fell off the roof, landing on top of a parked tank. "Good looking, my nigga," Billie said, as Nicole watched the soldier with his name over it slid into the building and started up the stairs with his M16 shooting anything that got in his way.

Nicole laughed. "Y'all really be into this damn game, huh?"

Billie shrugged his shoulders. "Cola, it's like real war and really being there!"

Nicole giggled. "Okay, Daddy," she said, getting up and about to go take her shower when she noticed his dick had gotten hard while she was rubbing his leg. Nicole ran her hand over it through his sweats. "Hmmmm, I see somebody is still moved by my touch." Nicole massaged his dick while Billie still yelled out orders. Nicole made his dick rise to its full ten inches, then pulled down the front of his sweats and before he could stop her, she grabbed his dick and placed it in her mouth.

"De'Shawn, get behind that—. Oooh shit," Billie moaned, his orders cut off as he felt his dick engulfed in her mouth.

Nicole kept stroking him as she bobbed her head up and down, enjoying distracting him.

"Damn, bitch," Billie moaned, while taking his headset off and throwing it toward the TV. He dropped his wireless remote then placed his hand on the back of Nicole's head, massaging her neck as she worked her throat and jaw.

On TV, the soldier with Billie's name over it had been shot. Slurping sounds and soft moans escaped Nicole's mouth as she sucked his dick as if her life depended on it.

"Ooh, Cola," Billie moaned as his eyes rolled in the back of his head. He placed his free hand into the front of her jeans and began rubbing her clit with his index and middle fingers. In one quick motion, Billie began rubbing her clit with his thumb and now was sliding his index and middle fingers in and out of her pussy.

Nicole, now grinding on Billie's fingers, began moaning louder, her pussy dripping wet. Nicole relaxed the muscles in her throat until his dick hit the back of her throat. Nicole tightened her mouth around his dick then started sucking with her lips and tongue.

"Ooooh, my fucking lord," Billie moaned as his toes curled.

Nicole pulled his dick slowly out of her mouth, grabbed the base and began bobbing her head up and down while stroking him with her free hand. Nicole slid his sweats and boxers down and began massaging his balls while still sucking his dick. Billie was moaning her name, which was making her pussy even wetter. He started tugging her pants off her hips. Nicole gladly wiggled her hips, still sucking his dick. She wanted him to have full access to her pussy and by the way he was pulling at her jeans, she knew that was just what Billie wanted as well.

Downstairs, Tasha had put the greens on the stove, placed the chicken in the fryer, made a pitcher of pink lemonade, but couldn't for the life of her figure out how to turn on the oven. A touch screen that talked every time she would hit a button, but it wouldn't ask her what her command was. Tasha would push in 260 degrees, but nothing would happen.

"Fuck this modern shit," Tasha stated out loud, wishing she could strangle the stove.

Command not recognized! Tasha rolled her eyes at the stove, and then gave it the bird. "Recognize that," she said, as she headed upstairs to ask Nicole how to operate the oven.

Half way up, Tasha heard moans from Nicole and Billie. Tasha started to go back down the stairs, but curiosity got the best of her. She walked to the top of the stairs, and then crept down the hall toward the sounds. The door was partially opened so she stepped to the side so she couldn't be seen, but still could see in the room.

When Tasha looked inside, she got more than an eyeful as she the biggest, smoothest and best-looking dick she'd ever seen. It was a perfectly made dick. Tasha's pussy instantly got wet and began to throb. She noticed how Billie's head was back and knew he was enjoying getting his dick and balls sucked. Imagining it was her giving him the pleasure, her pussy got even wetter. Tasha watched Nicole as she stood up slowly, pulling Billie's dick out her mouth, inch by inch, while still stroking his dick even after it was completely out of her mouth. Billie's fingers had not stopped working on Nicole's clit and she was letting out moans of pure pleasure. Tasha could not take her eyes off Billie's dick as Nicole stroked it up and down. It was the color of a Snicker's bar and glistened with Nicole's saliva.

Tasha could no longer control her body's hunger. She stuck her hand underneath her dress and began playing with her clit, never taking her eyes off Billie's dick.

"Ooh my God," Tasha moaned through clenched teeth as she replaced Nicole with herself in her mind while she began moving her finger faster on her clit keeping up with Nicole's strokes.

Billie turned Nicole around slowly, which caused her to let go of his dick as he guided her down on his dick. Billie wanted to watch Nicole's ass bounce up and down as she rode him.

Tasha had a clear view and watched as Nicole's pussy hungrily ate all ten inches of Billie's dick. Tasha let out a moan at the same time Nicole did when she had all ten inches of Billie's dick inside her. Tasha slipped two fingers inside her wet pussy still watching as Nicole bounced up and down on Billie's dick as if she was on a pogo stick while Billie gripped her hips.

"*Ooooh weeee*, Daddy, this is yo' pussy. *Oooh*, God, it's yours. *Oooohh*, Billie, *fuck* this pussy," Nicole moaned, riding Billie as he thrust his hips upward.

"Whose bitch are you?" he asked, smacking her on the ass.

"*Ooohh*, Daddy, I'm yo bitch, *I'm your* motherfuckin' bitch! *Ooohh shit*, Daddy, I'm *cuming*! Oooh, *Billie*, I'm cumming, Daddy," Nicole yelled as her body convulsed. "*Ahh, shit!* she moaned still shaking as Billie continued to bring her up and down off his dick with each thrust.

In the hallway, Tasha pushed a third finger inside her pussy. She was watching the thrust Billie was giving Nicole. "*Ohh*, my God, Billie, I'm about to cum." Tasha moaned a little louder than she meant to; she was so gone she didn't even stop to see if they heard her or not. Tasha spread her legs wider using three fingers as if they were Billie's dick. Tasha began shaking. "*Oooooh, shit!* Oooh, my goodness," she moaned as Billie started slamming harder into Nicole.

"*Oooooh, Daddy*," Nicole moaned. "I love you! I'ma cum again."

Billie heard something in the hallway. He continued to move Nicole up and down on his dick. He thought he was tripping, then he heard a moan, which didn't come from Nicole. He raised his head and saw a shadow. Billie felt Nicole's walls tighten on his dick and lost focus on the hallway as his dick began throbbing and he shot his load inside of Nicole's pussy.

"*Oooooh*, bitch, I love you," Billie moaned.

Tasha had cum twice while watching them fuck. The first time she kept her eyes opened, watching every single movement they made. Tasha came so hard she almost screamed. The second time Tasha got so caught up in her fantasy of it being her riding Billie's dick instead of Nicole that she closed her eyes and began ramming her fingers deep inside her pussy. Her juices were running down her fingers and thighs when she finally stopped shaking and was able to open her eyes. Tasha took her fingers out of her pussy. They were dripping with her juices. *Damn,* she thought to herself, realizing that she just had one of the best orgasms she'd ever had in her life.

Tasha adjusted her dress and then sucked her juices off her fingers, imagining her fingers were Billie's dick. Tasha caught eye contact with Billie through the crack of the door. She jumped back, then slowly looked again through the door. Billie was now facing Nicole. Tasha giggled to herself, knowing that she hadn't been seen.

Tasha quickly moved down the hallway and descended the stairs. Once back in the kitchen, a huge smile came across her face, as she washed her hands. *I ain't even got none of that nigga's dick and his punk ass got me sprung.* Tasha laughed to herself, deciding to try the oven one more time.

Please enter your command!

"I'ma set this oven at 260 degrees if it kills me," Tasha stated while playing with the touch screen.

Voice command accepted!

"Voice command accepted!" Tasha said to herself as the lights came on in the oven and it began to heat up. "Voice command!" Tasha started laughing. "Ain't this about a bitch?

This motherfucker is voice activated." She stuck the cornbread in the oven, still laughing. "I'll be damned," she said, closing the oven door and then started setting the table. "I'll be goddamned..."

CHAPTER 4

NICOLE CAME DOWNSTAIRS THEN WENT INTO the kitchen feeling like a new woman. She had just got dicked down and was smiling from ear to ear.

"Damn, bitch, what you so happy about?" Tasha asked, but already knew why.

"I'm just happy. That's okay right?" Nicole stated, still smiling.

"Hell yeah it's okay, especially when you living like the queen you are and also being treated like one as well," Tasha said while taking the Cornbread out the oven.

"Girl, the food is ready. Where is Billie's crazy ass?"

"He is still upstairs in that game room," Nicole said, while jogging to the bottom of stairs. "Daddy, the food is ready," she yelled up the stairs, then walked back to the kitchen. They heard him coming down the stairs, two at a time.

"Well, it's about damn time," Billie stated as he entered the kitchen, rubbing his stomach.

Tasha's pussy began to tingle when she saw Billie. Tasha didn't realize she was staring at him.

"Tee, what the fuck are you staring at?" Billie asked with a smirk on his face, now staring at her.

Tasha rolled her eyes. "Shit, I was trying to figure out what wild animal yo momma mated with to make yo funny looking ass!"

Nicole started laughing, and Tasha joined her.

Billie smiled. "Ha ha ha, you got jokes, huh, Ms. last comic standing? But just in case you can't figure it out, try calling your mom and asking her stanky ass, because I'm sure she knows the answer since me and you have the same Daddy!"

Both Tasha and Nicole's mouth fell open as Billie started laughing.

"Fuck you!" Tasha pushed Billie and sat down at the table.

"Oh, you can dish it out, but yo ass can't take it?" Billie said, still laughing.

Pouting, Tasha crossed her arms over her chest. Nicole took up for her friend and popped Billie in the back of the head.

"Uh, what was that for?" he asked with a frown. "She started it!"

They all started laughing.

"Y'all both some big babies," Nicole said, putting the food on the table. "Now enough of the bullshit, a bitch is hungry, let's eat."

After they finished eating, they sat at the table joking around and recalling old times. Billie received a call from a private contractor who wanted to meet with him so they could close a business deal. Billie owned his own plumbing company. Since it opened in 2003, he hadn't looked back. He was now one of the most asked about plumbing companies when it came to large jobs in the Los Angeles area.

Billie kissed Nicole, then gave Tasha a hug. "I'll see y'all later. I, more than likely, will be back home in an hour or so. This shouldn't take long."

Billie grabbed his keys to his 2012 Jaguar and went out the front door.

Nicole started cleaning the table as Tasha loaded the dishwasher. After she cut the dishwasher on, Tasha wiped off the stove and counters before taking a seat at the table with Nicole.

"So what's good?" Tasha asked as Nicole sipped on a glass of pink lemonade.

"Shit, nothing as far as I can see. I'm ready to hit the mall if you want it. You know Macy's is having that 60% off sale, so why wait 'til Saturday? Billie's gone to a meeting. He won't be back for at least an hour or more, so let's do us!"

Tasha was with whatever, whenever, when it came to her girl Nicole. "That sounds good to me, but before we hit the mall, let me go home and change clothes. You can pick me up from my house!"

"Bitch, what? You don't like my dress?" Nicole asked, smiling.

"Naw, ho, it ain't that. A bitch needs some clean underwear on before she steps out. As of now, I have on a bra, but no panties and you know I don't roll like that. But just so you know, I'm planning on keeping this dress and the shoes; that's how much I like it so you can count it as one of my many birthday gifts." Tasha grinned, with her hands on her hips.

"Bitch, that's Prada, that's all you'll be getting for the next three years!"

They shared a laugh, then hugged as Tasha stood up.

"Meet me at my house in an hour, I love you!"

They embraced again.

"Bitch, I love you, too," Nicole replied now walking Tasha to the door.

After Tasha was gone, Nicole sat down on the sofa in the living room, grabbed the remote to the Bose system and put on the Drake, *I Care* CD. As the music began to play through the speakers, Nicole started thinking of how lucky she was to have a man who truly loved her like Billie did, and also a best friend who was like a sister to her.

Nicole wanted to give Billie kids, but the doctor told them that she would not be able to have children. Well to be exact, his words were, "You have a very low chance of ever conceiving," which meant the same thing to both her and Billie. Nicole knew Billie wanted kids and thought he would leave her after he had heard this from the doctor. They had been trying to have a baby for two years. Billie has assumed it was him that was the reason why they had taken the trip to the doctor's office. That was over three years ago when they found out she couldn't have children and they still were together, standing strong and now in their first home. *God will bless us with a child, I have faith in my Lord.* Nicole exhaled as her favorite song on Drake's CD, "Take a Shot For Me," played softly through the speakers.

Nicole thought about Tasha. They had been friends since she could remember. She and Tasha had done everything together; they hung together like sisters. Their mothers were best friends before they were born and now they were best friends. They knew more about each other than they knew about themselves. Nicole laughed to herself. "Me and that bitch have done some crazy shit," she stated out loud, as she got up and headed up the stairs.

Once upstairs, Nicole took off her clothes in her bedroom, then went into the bathroom to take a shower. *Let me start getting ready because knowing Tee, she's probably already waiting for me.* Nicole hopped in the shower, closed the door and grabbed her favorite shower nozzle— the vibrator. Tasha made it home in ten minutes flat. Stripping off her clothes as she walked through her front door, she couldn't get Billie or his dick out of her mind. Tasha was really trippin', because a nigga never in her life could rent space in her head and the first nigga that was finally able to do it was her best friend's man.

Damn it, why the fuck didn't he ever pay me any attention in school? she asked herself as she walked into her bathroom to take a quick shower. Tasha thought back to when they were all in middle school, and she had five of her six classes with Billie. They would always sit next to each other, joking and talking about other students in their classes, but somehow their conversation would always end up being about Nicole. They would talk about things they had in common and places they both liked to go or movies they enjoyed and out of nowhere, he'd say, "So, what's up with your friend Nicole?"

Tasha stepped out of the shower, grabbed a towel and began drying herself off.

"Naw, nigga, the question should have been, 'What was up with you and me?'" she said angrily as she threw the towel across the bathroom.

Tasha liked Billie from day one. Nicole had always brushed him off as just another annoying boy, until finally one day, listening to Tasha's advice, she just decided to go out on one date with him so he would stop asking about her and leave her alone. Well, after that one date in the ninth grade, they have been inseparable.

Yeah, nigga, you got a good bitch, but you could have had a little bit better! Tasha thought to herself as she put on a pair of G-string panties and a bra. She put lotion on her body then slipped into a pair of 7 Jeans with a ruffle, laced top. Tasha grabbed her seven-inch heels.

"You could have had me," she said out loud, as her house phone rung.

No one had her house number, but her job, Nicole, her mother, Nicole's mom and Billie. Tasha hoped it was Billie, but knew it wasn't. She snatched the phone off the hook, answering it with an attitude.

"HELLO?"

"Damn, bitch, who you mad at?" Nicole asked, hearing how her best friend answered the phone.

"Bitch, you, what's up?" Tasha shot back.

Nicole started laughing. Tasha couldn't help but laugh as well at her own true statement.

"Well, if it helps any, I'm sorry I kept yo crazy ass waiting, bitch, but I'm pulling up to your house now, so, bitch, get ready to step out."

"Ho, you know I stay ready. I'm walking out the door as we speak. I'll see you in a second!"

Tasha hung up the phone and grabbed her purse, still laughing to herself on how she had let it slip that she was mad at Nicole for a reason Nicole knew nothing about.

Damn, this nigga got me whipped and ain't even touched me. I won't never clown my girl again about being sprung! Tasha though to herself as she locked her front door, and walked down her walkway to Nicole's 2012 Jaguar that matched Billie's.

Tasha got in the car, slamming the door. "Bitch, you just don't know how much I love you," Tasha stated as she threw her purse in the back seat.

Nicole looked over at her, smiling. "Ho, I was just thinking the same thing." They started laughing.

"Whatever, bitch," Tasha said looking through the CD holder. "Let's go spend some money!" They pulled from the curve subbing Rick Ross, "My Bitch Bad," looking like a bag of money.

CHAPTER 5

BILLIE'S MEETING ENDED SOONER THAN HE expected. It was a complicated deal, but he closed it in record time. There was a WalMart being built in downtown Compton. He would do all the plumbing for the whole building for the sum of $875,000. He was excited! This was his highest paying job yet. Almost a ticket. *Damn a nigga really done made it out of the gutter,* Billie thought as he pulled into the drive-thru of Tams Burger Stand on Rosecrans and Central. He ordered a pastrami special with a side of onion rings and a medium pineapple shake. He got his food and then hopped on the 105 Freeway to the 405. He thought about the shadow that he saw when he and Nicole were fucking in his game room. Billie could have even sworn he heard a moan.

"Tasha was in that hallway watching us fuck," he said out

loud, as he exited the 405 on LaTijera. His dick got hard off the idea of Tasha watching him and Nicole fuck.

As he pulled into his driveway, he thought about all the fantasies he'd had of a threesome with Nicole and Tasha. Billie chuckled as he put the car in park and turned off the ignition. *I'm letting my mind play tricks on me because I knew she was in the house while it was going down.* Billie grabbed his food and exited his car. As he unlocked his front door and walked into his house, he shook his head, grinning. *I have enough problems to deal with already; I can't be letting my head create new ones!* He closed and locked the door and went into the kitchen, sat down at the table and started eating his food. He noticed a note Nicole had left on the table and read it while eating an onion ring.

> *Daddy, if you beat me home, I'm at the Del Amo Mall with Tasha.*
>
> *We will be back soon. Skype me if you want to. I love you, so smile.* ☺
>
> *Love, Cola*

Billie smiled after finishing the note. "I got a good bitch," he said, then took a bite of his pastrami sandwich. He finished his food and decided he would take a nap until Nicole got home. As he headed up the stairs, a flashback of Tasha standing at the glass doors wearing no bra came to mind. *Yeah, that's what it was,* he told himself as he took a sip of his shake. *I saw her half naked and that's what took my mind there with that shadow shit!* Billie chuckled again. *Can you blame a nigga?* He remembered how mouthwatering Tasha breasts looked when she was at the glass doors next to Nicole, whose breasts were looking just as good. He sat his shake down on the nightstand.

"Hell naw, you can't," he said, grinning, as he decided to Skype Nicole so he could get her best friend out of his mind. Billie looked through his phone, found his Skype App, then hit *View Cola with Conversation* and hit send. He waited for a few seconds before the Skype acknowledged there was no answer. Billie tried to call straight through. Nicole didn't pick up that time either. Worried, Billie went through his Skype contacts, found Tasha's number, and then hit send.

Tasha was in Fredrick's of Hollywood trying on a see-through nightie when her phone went off. She noticed it was a Skype and picked up the phone to see who it was. Tasha began smiling when she saw it was Billie. She didn't have on a bra or any panties. Tasha accepted the Skype.

"What up, big head?" Tasha said, holding the phone so that he could only see her face.

"Uh, what's up, Tee, is Nicole right by you? I tried to Skype and call her, but she didn't answer so I got worried and called you!"

Tasha sucked her teeth. "Nigga, you know we fine," she said, smiling. "You always worrying with your over protective ass. Hold on, I'ma hand her the phone!"

"Thanks, Tee, and I ain't over protective either!"

"Whatever, big head. Like I said, hold on!" Tasha's pussy got wet just hearing Billie's voice. She wished he were being over protective of her. She stuck her arm outside her dressing room door with the phone in her hand.

"Here, yo nigga on the phone worried about you!" Tasha closed the door after Nicole took the phone.

"Hey, Daddy, what's good?" Nicole asked with a Kool-Aid smile.

"Shit, missing you, are you okay? Why you not answering your phone?" Billie asked with concern in his voice.

Nicole looked on her phone clip that was on her purse, noticing it wasn't there. "Ooh shit, Daddy I'm sorry. My phone is down in my purse. I put it in there after I got off the phone with my mom and was trying on some clothes."

"Okay baby, 'cause you know how I am when it comes to you. You're my heart!"

"I know, Daddy," Nicole said smiling. "You know you're mine, too!"

"How's Moms?" Billie asked.

"She's good. She asked when we are going to stop by and spend some time with her. I told her probably next weekend."

"Yeah, that sounds good. I haven't seen her in a week, yo moms is the craziest!"

"Yeah, she loves you, too, and told me to tell you that!"

"Well, Cola, I was just calling to check up on you and let you know I made it home so whenever y'all done, you need to get yo ass here so we can finish what you started earlier."

Nicole laughed. "Nigga, you ain't said nothing but a word. I'll be home in an hour."

"Yeah, get yo ass here because Daddy got something for you."

Nicole giggled. "Oooh and I want it all, too, every single inch of it!" They shared a laugh. "I love you, Daddy!"

"I love you, Cola. I'ma take a quick shower, and I'll see you when you get here." He blew her a kiss, ended the call and placed the phone on the dresser.

Nicole knocked on the dressing room door, handing Tasha back her phone. Tasha opened the door sticking out her head and hand at the same time.

"Bitch, we need to hurry up. I got some unfinished business at home I need to take care of," Nicole said with a smirk on her face.

"Umm hmm, I bet." Tasha said smiling. "Give me a few more minutes." Tasha closed the dressing room door then looked at her phone. The Skype was still connected. Tasha could see Nicole's bedroom on her screen. She smiled as she saw Billie taking off his shirt. A wicked and devilish thought went through Tasha's mind. She sat her phone down on the chair, angling it so that Billie would be able to see her whole body and she started singing "Every Girl In the World" by Lil Wayne and Drake.

Billie heard singing coming from his phone and looked over at the nightstand, realizing the Skype was still connected. He walked over to disconnect the line and saw Tasha trying on lingerie. He jumped out the view of his camera so that she wouldn't see him, but kept his eyes on his screen, watching her closely. Tasha was standing in front of the mirror in a see-through, pink nightie, running her hand over her breasts, which was making her nipples hard. Billie's dick got hard as steel as he watched Tasha do a three-sixty spin in the mirror, looking at herself. Tasha wasn't paying attention to the phone so Billie assumed he was at fault for not disconnecting the Skype, but Tasha knew what she was doing. Tasha wanted him to see what he could've had. She took the nightie off her shoulders, letting it drop to the floor and stood in front of the mirror, completely naked. Billie could see Tasha's beautiful, full breasts, flat stomach and shaved pussy through the reflection in the mirror; her body was flawless. From the view of the camera, he could see her perfectly shaped ass. Tasha bent over at the waist, spreading her legs a little, giving Billie a view of her pussy from the back while she slowly picked up the nightie. Tasha took her sweet time standing upright, and then placed the nightie on its hanger. Billie's dick was so hard he thought it would explode.

"Damn Tee," he said out loud, but then quickly covered his mouth, remembering Tasha could hear him.

Tasha, feeling she had accomplished her goal, put her panties on seductively and slowly, facing the camera and then did the same with her bra, making sure the phone didn't miss a second of her actions. She then grabbed her 7 Jeans, pulled them over her hips and placed her shirt on, buttoning it up slowly as she slipped her feet in her shoes. Tasha grabbed her purse and the lingerie she had tried on as she opened the dressing room door and walked out, leaving her phone behind on purpose.

Billie's dick was so hard it was causing him pain. He knew for sure without any doubt that he was going to have even more fantasies of Tasha now and he wanted to fuck the shit out of her right at that moment. Billie looked at his phone, realizing Tasha had left her phone in the dressing room. He was about to call Nicole, but decided not to because if he told her Tasha left her phone, Tasha would realize that he had been watching her while she was in the dressing room and she would more than likely tell Nicole. There would be no way to explain why he didn't disconnect the Skype. Just as he was trying to figure out a way to let her know about her phone without exposing his watching her, Tasha walked back in the dressing room. Billie once again moved out of the view of the camera on his phone.

Tasha looked around the dressing room as if she'd lost something. Seeing her phone she smiled, yelling, "I found it, Cola. I left it in the dressing room!"

Tasha looked at her screen and Billie wanted to dive under the bed. "Ooohh shit, it's still connected," Tasha said out loud. She picked up the phone. "Hello. Hello. Billie, are you there?" she said, looking into the camera. "Ooh well," she said, shrugging her shoulders after not getting a reply.

Tasha played with the phone for a few seconds and Billie saw his screen go black, followed by a text message stating: *Your Skype call has been ended.* Billie exhaled; he'd been holding his breath since Tasha walked back in the dressing room.

He grabbed his phone as soon as he saw that Tasha had disconnected the Skype and fell on his bed. His dick was still hard as he thought about what he had just witnessed. Visions of Tasha's body were running through his head. *Damn, Tee got a fat ass pussy*, he thought, as he pictured himself holding on to Tasha's hips, hitting that pussy from the back. His dick throbbed from the thought.

Billie jumped off the bed. *Fuck this, I need a drink*, he thought as he walked down the stairs, his dick leading the way. Once in the kitchen, he poured a glass of Patron and downed it. Billie went back upstairs and into his game room. A nap was out of the question. He needed to ease his mind. He turned on the PS3, put on the headset, grabbed the controller and started playing his favorite game.

Tasha was on cloud nine. She knew what she had done and knew Billie had seen her. Tasha saw him trying to duck out of the way of the camera as she was in the mirror.

"Bitch, what you smirking about?" Nicole asked, breaking Tasha's train of thought. Nicole was eyeing her best friend suspiciously, waiting for an answer.

"Nothing, I'm just thinking about something." Tasha's face still held a devilish smirk.

"Now, bitch, I know you and I also know that smirk, so go on somewhere with that bullshit. What yo ass done did?"

Tasha rolled her eyes and laughed. "Okay, bitch, damn! I walked out of Fredrick's with a teddy under my clothes that cost $2,900," she lied.

"See, bitch, I knew you did something crazy." Nicole laughed. "I can't wait to see it," Nicole stated, still laughing.

"Yeah, it's one of those must-have-it-by-any-means-necessary because it is one of a kind. That's why I took it," Tasha said as they exited the mall, with the smirk still on her face.

Tasha was amazed at how easy she had come up with a lie to tell her best friend. She was hoping she had left a lasting impression on Billie's mind as he had left on hers. "Yeah, now we even," Tasha said out loud as they got to the car, not realizing she had just voiced her thoughts.

"Ah, hell naw, bitch, you talking to yo'self now?" Nicole said, looking at Tasha over the top of the car as she unlocked the doors for them to get in. "Yeah, I'm taking yo ass to a psychiatrist fo' sho!"

They started laughing as they got in the car, closed the doors and pulled off and out the mall parking lot. Little did Nicole know, her man was getting mind fucked.

CHAPTER 6

Nicole dropped Tasha off and headed home. Billie's Jag was parked in the driveway instead of the garage. She parked her Jag next to his. Nicole grabbed her shopping bags and her purse and hopped out of the car, and headed toward the front door.

As she entered the house, she could hear Black Ops 2 playing upstairs. Nicole smiled as she closed and locked the door. "I'm about to make him forget all about that punk ass game," she said, looking through her bags. Once Nicole found what she was looking for, she took the items out the bag and sat her purse by the front door.

Once upstairs, Nicole took off her clothes, including her panties and bra, slipped on the nightie she'd chosen out of the bag. Nicole crossed the hallway, went into the game room and walked in front of the TV. She placed her left hand on her hip and adjusted her weight.

"So what do you think?" Nicole asked as the TV shone through the nightie, revealing her beautiful, curvy body.

Billie's mouth fell open while his mind raced. *This gotta be a setup*, he thought, his dick now erect like a pole, making his pajama pants look like a pop-up tent. In front of him his girl was wearing the exact same nightie Tasha had worn earlier in the dressing room on Skype.

Nicole smiled, loving his reaction. She seductively walked over to him, placing her index finger on his chin, closing his mouth as she knocked the controller out of his hand.

"Play times over, Daddy. Now what is it that you have for me?"

Billie was looking at Nicole, but all he could he see was Tasha. He licked his lips as his dick began throbbing.

"I'ma give you what you want, bitch," Billie said in a lustful tone that even he didn't recognize. With lust-filled eyes, he stood up, ripping his pajama pants from his body.

Nicole, shocked at his strength, giggled as she was picked up and carried out of the game room and into their bedroom. Without a word, he laid her down on their bed then quickly removed his shirt. Nicole scooted up toward the headboard, never taking her eyes off of him. She was turned on by the beast that had taken over her man.

Billie climbed up on the bed, and began sucking Nicole's toes.

"Oooh shit," Nicole moaned, feeling chills run through her body as he took his time licking, then sucking each one of her toes.

Billie, now finished with her toes, began running his tongue up her leg, planting soft kisses in some spots, while lightly sucking on others as he got to Nicole's thighs. She gladly parted them for him. Billie used his two index fingers to open the lips of her pussy and began licking and sucking on Nicole's clit.

"Oooh shit, aaahhh, Billie," Nicole screamed as he ate her pussy as if it was his last meal. Billie sucked her clit like a newborn sucking on a baby bottle. Billie felt Nicole's legs shake; he eased off her clit and started flicking his tongue in and out of her pussy, which had Nicole about to pull out her hair. She was moaning and saying his name so loud she knew everyone on the block heard her.

Billie ate Nicole's pussy for thirty minutes before letting up. Nicole had cum three times, her mind was blank and she was in a daze. Her legs were shaking uncontrollably as Billie began planting soft kisses on her stomach as he worked his way up to her nipples. He used two fingers to slide her nightie off her shoulders as he placed her left nipple in his mouth, sucking it 'til it was completely hard before moving to the right nipple, doing the same. Nicole ran her hands over his back, moaning loudly; her pussy was so wet it could have been mistaken for a Slip 'N Slide. Billie let go of her right nipple, working his tongue up to her neck, as he began sucking and placing soft kisses.

Hovering over her, he looked her in the eyes and then began kissing her lips. Nicole parted her lips and their tongues danced. Nicole loved how his tongue tasted and let out moans of pleasure as they kissed and he sucked her top lip, then her bottom lip before breaking the kiss and placing soft kisses on her face. He reached her ear, sucking on her earlobe, and whispered, "I'ma fuck the shit out of you."

Nicole moaned, "Please!"

He rolled her on her stomach and began running his tongue down the center of her back. When he got to her ass, he parted her cheeks and ran his tongue around Nicole's asshole, then began sliding his tongue in and out of it.

"Ohhhhh, my God," she moaned as goose bumps rose all over her body. Nicole almost passed out from the sensation and pleasure she was feeling. "Oooh, Daddy, that *feels so good*," she moaned as his tongue-fucked her asshole. It was feeling so good to Nicole that she began grinding her ass on his tongue. Billie let her enjoy it for a few more minutes, before turning her back over on her back. Mentally, Billie was fucking Tasha, giving her what he knew she wanted. Billie slowly entered Nicole as she wrapped her legs around his waist. Nicole screamed his name as all ten inches of his dick slid inside her tight, wet pussy. Billie brought his dick in and out of Nicole until her walls had gotten used to his dick. He then removed her legs from his waist, placing them on his shoulders and began ramming his dick in and out of Nicole. Nicole worked her hips in a circular motion, meeting his thrusts.

"Yeah, bitch, is this what you wanted?" Billie asked between clinched teeth.

"Ooooh yes, Daddy, *oooh, yes, ahhhh,*" Nicole moaned as Billie tried to fuck her back out. Nicole could feel his dick in her stomach on each inward thrust. She let out moans of sheer pleasure as he went deeper and deeper. Her body started shaking uncontrollably. Nicole screamed out in ecstasy as she had a gut-wrenching orgasm. Billie pulled his dick out of Nicole after she stopped shaking.

"Now, turn over," Billie commanded.

By the time Nicole had gathered her senses and realized what he wanted her to do, Billie was helping her to obey. Nicole looked over her shoulders as he placed a pillow under her stomach, which propped up her ass.

"Arch your back," Billie said as Nicole continued looking over her shoulder. Seeing his dick covered in her juices made her pussy throb. She arched her back and Billie entered her. He grabbed Nicole's hips and rammed himself so hard into her that she lost her breath.

"*Oooh, Billie, oooh, weessuss, Daddy,* it's yours. *Oooh, God,* it's yours," Nicole moaned then bit into a pillow as she felt another orgasm about to consume her. Nicole's body began jerking wildly as she had the orgasm of her life. Cum ran down her legs and thighs as well as down Billie's dick and balls. Nicole was still trying to catch her breath when she felt Billie sliding his dick into her ass.

"Oooh, Daddy, please I can't take no more! Aaaahhh," Nicole moaned as her sentence was cut off by his dick entering her asshole. "Ooohhhh, Daddy, B-I-L-L-I-E, ooooohhhhh, B-I-L-L-I-E," Nicole moaned as Billie slowly worked his dick in and out of her ass. When he felt her muscles in her ass adjust to his dick, he started pounding in and out of her rectum. Billie had a grip on Nicole's hips and was driving his dick so deep in her ass that she thought it was coming out of her mouth.

"Whose bitch are you?" Billie asked through clinched teeth, and then slapped Nicole on her ass.

"*I'm…your…bitch…Daddy*," Nicole said in between moans. She felt Billie speed up and knew he was about to cum.

That gave her the strength she needed. Nicole wanted to please Billie as he had pleased her. Nicole arched her back bringing her ass up further, meeting his thrust. She began rocking her body backward and forward as he went out of her rectum.

"Ooohhh, Daddy hit this ass. Oooohhh, Billie, cum for Mommie. Uuuummmm, Daddy, cum in this tight ass!"

Billie gripped Nicole's hips tightly and, with a loud animal like roar, he unloaded what felt like a gallon of sperm inside of Nicole's ass. Nicole tightened her muscles around his dick as it released its load inside her. She felt Billie slowly pulling his dick out of her. She moaned softly as it completely exited her ass.

Nicole tried to move, but her body refused to respond. "Daddy," she called out as she reached for him. Billie moved up the bed and fell down next to her still breathing hard. "Ooohhh, God, Daddy, I love you," Nicole said as she placed her hand on his chest.

Billie placed an arm around her. "I love you, too, Cola." He kissed her on the forehead. They both drifted off to sleep in each other's arms.

Nicole was awakened by the sound of her cellphone vibrating. It stopped then started again. Just as she thought the caller had gotten the message that no one was going to answer, the house phone began ringing. *Damn*, she thought, as she got out of bed trying to get to the phone before it woke up Billie. Nicole tried to walk her normal stride but couldn't. She giggled. Billie had fucked the shit out of her, literally. Nicole made it to the phone on the third ring, snatching it off the base.

"Hello," she said, whispering into the receiver.

"Hey, bitch, what's up?" Tasha asked, sounding wide-awake.

"Shit nothing, laid up, why you calling so late, is everything okay?" Nicole asked with concern in her voice.

"Bitch, it's only 11:20 pm. What the fuck you on?" Tasha laughed.

"Damn, bitch, I thought it was like two or three in the morning. See what good dick will do to you?" Nicole said with a giggle.

Tasha sucked her teeth. "What the fuck whatever," she said with an attitude.

"No, for real, bitch, after I came home, I put on that nightie you picked out for me and girl it drove Billie crazy. That nigga fucked the shit out of me; got a bitch walking funny and all that!"

Hearing that, a smile crossed Tasha's face without her even realizing it.

"I told you he would like it," Tasha replied, still smiling. "Anyway, I think I left one of my bags in your car, that's the reason I called."

"It's the bag with the purple and white, two-piece, see-through negligee set," Nicole said, holding it up with the phone on her shoulder.

"Yeah, bitch, I know; that's why I'm calling about it. I was going through my shit and couldn't find it. That set cost a bitch $200.00. If you didn't have it, I was going to skip work or be late so I could go up to Del Amo mall first thing in the morning."

Nicole started laughing. "Bitch, you really can't trip if they acted like they didn't know what you was talking about because you come up on them anyway."

Tasha took the phone away from her ear and looked at it with a frown, and then returned it to her ear. "Bitch, I ain't getting over going back after some shit I paid for," she replied with an attitude.

Nicole started laughing loudly. "Bitch, don't even try to front with that attitude, yo ass did get over by stealing that $290.00 piece you walked out with underneath your clothes without paying for it, so you can stop fronting and acting brand new because these phones ain't bugged or tapped."

Tasha had forgotten about the lie she had told when they were at the mall. She began laughing, trying to play it off. "Okay, bitch, damn I was hoping you forgot about that!"

"Naw, bitch, I ain't forgot a damn thang and I'm dying to see what it looks like. It gotta be all that if you pulled an old grab and go move," Nicole said, giggling.

Tasha started laughing, reminiscing about how they used to do their thang when they were younger. "Bitch, remember that time we tried to walk out of Wilson's House of Suede and Leather with those bomber jackets on?"

Nicole was now laughing too. "Yeah I remember, but we didn't try, you tried. I made it to the door, so I succeeded. Yo ass kept looking back, that's why you and only you got caught. I got outside the door and started running when I didn't see you running next to me. I stopped and looked back; there you were in the middle of two men in suits looking at me all poppy-eyed and shit through the door you never made it out of. Well shit, I was watching" Nicole laughed.

"Naw, bitch, yo ass was scared, but the fucked up part is that it was your idea!"

They were laughing uncontrollably.

"Bitch, we got our asses whipped that night," Nicole recalled. Thinking about how Tasha's mom had picked them up and whipped them, then after her mom got off work, she came to Tasha's house, got the run down from Tasha's mom, then took her home and whipped her ass again.

"Yeah, bitch, because of you, we got our asses whipped, but I got one beat down, yo ass got two...and I still had a jacket," Tasha teased in between laughs.

"Whatever, ho, so what?" Nicole giggled. "Bitch, I love you!"

"Yeah, I love yo scary ass, too," Tasha replied,

"Look, Tee, I'll leave your bag in the living room. If I'm not here, use your key and pick it up. I'm about to get back to sleep. A bitch gotta go to work in the morning."

"Yeah, I'ma hit the sheets, too. I'll see you tomorrow!"

"Okay, talk to you later, good night, Tee!"

"Night, Cola!"

Nicole hung up the phone, still thinking of some of the adventures her and Tasha had been through. Nicole got back in bed with Billie and looked him over while he slept. He looked so at peace, like a sleeping baby.

"I don't know what got in yo ass tonight, but you put it down on me," Nicole said in a very low tone. She kissed him softly on the lips. "Nigga, I love you. Yo ass gonna marry me!" Nicole looked down at his dick and cleared her throat. "Because I'm sharing that with nobody. It's all mine. You got a bitch ready to sign them papers." She giggled as she rested her head on his chest. Within minutes, Nicole was asleep wearing a Kool-Aid smile her face.

CHAPTER 7

AFTER NICOLE HUNG UP THE PHONE, Tasha held the receiver tightly in her hand for a few minutes lost in thought. Tasha knew that she would be on Billie's mind from the stunt she pulled in the dressing room at Fredrick's of Hollywood. She also knew that when he saw that pink nightie in Nicole's closet or on her, he would have a flashback causing him to think about her even more. Tasha, however, had no idea, nor did she plan on Nicole wearing the nightie tonight.

The phone started making a loud beeping noise from being off the hook; the sound snapped Tasha out of her trance. She placed the phone on its base and then smiled.

"I wonder if he was thinking about me while he was fucking her," Tasha said out loud, as she walked to her bedroom.

Since she lived alone, she always walked around the house naked or in a wife beater with nothing underneath it. Tasha sat on her California King-sized bed as she thought about what she was doing and started feeling guilty for her actions. Then she thought back to middle school and how she was always was there for Billie and how she always wanted him. Tasha smiled as she remembered back to when he needed someone to talk to about this girl or that girl, or her best friend, Nicole; he always turned to her.

"I should have told his ass how I felt," Tasha said, realizing that it was her fault for never speaking up on how she felt about him in middle school. But, she did remember telling Nicole that she thought Billie was fine as hell and that she didn't know why she wouldn't give him a chance.

"Fuck," Tasha blurted, mad because she knew she couldn't have what she truly wanted, which was Billie. Tasha loved Nicole like a sister; she couldn't let some childhood crush come between their bond and friendship.

I'ma stand down, she thought. *I can't let this keep going on, risking hurting my girl.*

Tasha laid back in her bed, deciding to keep her plot to seduce Billie to herself. *Whatever fantasies I have will have to stay just fantasies and between me, myself and I.* Tasha was cool until she saw them having sex. Her lust brought back all of her old feelings. Sure, she would think of how making love to him would be, but that was because of the stories Nicole would tell her. But it had never gotten to this point.

"Fuck," Tasha yelled at the top of her voice. "I should have never taken my nosey ass up those stairs." Tasha started remembering what she saw; her pussy became wet as she replayed the scene in her head. "Damn you, Billie, you black motherfucker!" She reached under her pillow, pulling out her four-and-a-half-inch dildo. She opened her legs as wide as she could. Then fucked herself with the dildo until she came. After two orgasms later, Tasha fell asleep thinking about riding Billie's dick.

* * *

Nicole woke up feeling brand new. She still couldn't walk the way she normally did but she didn't mind because she loved every minute of what had her walking differently. Nicole took a quick shower, put lotion on her body and then went to her closet to pick out an outfit for work. She decided on a loosely fitted summer dress so everyone at work wouldn't notice her new walk. Nicole smiled as she put on her panties and bra, thinking about how Billie had put it down on her last night. After Nicole finished dressing, she walked over to the bed and stood over Billie. He was still sound asleep. *I guess I put it on him, too*, Nicole thought, then giggled. Billie looked so peaceful that she decided to let him sleep. She knew he usually didn't go into his office till after 11:00 am, since he had a dependable secretary and a good lead man. Sometimes he wouldn't go in at all, and on those days he would do estimates, check on jobs that the crews were doing in different locations or go get needed supplies, and then head back home. Since it was only 7:30 am and Nicole knew he needed his rest, she decided to do just that, let him rest.

She kissed him softly on his lips. "I love you so, so much," she whispered as she pulled the covers over him.

As Nicole was walking down the stairs, she decided to cook Billie breakfast, since she still had forty-five minutes before she had to be at work. Nicole picked up her cell phone to text Tasha as she walked into the kitchen.

> *Hey Tee, good morning. I know you going to be working in the field today bitch, but I want to know I'ma miss yo crazy ass at work, a bitch hate having to drive 2 work alone, because I'm so use to your company, I love you and will see you at lunch time. Meet me at Red Lobsters on Crenshaw in the shopping center by Applebee's*

and Ross. Ooh yeah bitch, its your turn to pay
the tab (lol) talk to you later...
ur sis Cola

Nicole hit send, and then sat her phone on the counter as she got the eggs, bacon, sausage and biscuits out of the fridge. Her phone went off. Nicole set the food on the sink so she could read Tasha's text:

Yeah bitch, I'ma miss you too. I love when we
drive to work together as well, not only because
you my girl, but yo ass is funny as hell, and F.Y.I.
I didn't forget its my turn to pay the tab...Ho, you
the one that try to act brand new when its my turn
to pick the place to eat and you gotta pay with yo
cheap ass (smile), I'm not leaving the house till
like maybe 11am. I love I love my field days, a
bitch can get some well needed rest. I'll see you
at Red Lobster at 12:30. I love U 2
Lov yo sis, Tee

Nicole laughed. "Tasha's ass is crazy," she said, turning on the stove. She grabbed two pans from the dishwasher and went to work on cooking. It took her a total of fifteen minutes to make

Billie's breakfast. Nicole made his plate, wrapped it in foil then placed it in the oven. She looked at the clock on the stove and it read 7:54 AM. She had about twenty minutes before she had to be at work. Nicole stuck a piece of bacon in her mouth as she wrote Billie a quick note. When she finished, she ran upstairs and placed the note on the bathroom door, knowing that would be the first place he would go when he got up. She went over to the bed, gave him another kiss and went back downstairs to leave for work. Nicole grabbed her phone, car keys and house keys, placing everything in her purse as she walked out of the house.

Once outside, Nicole noticed it was misty. She decided to pull Billie's Jag in the garage for him, just in case it rained. Nicole did this as quickly as she could, knowing she was now pressed for time. She noticed Billie's digital clock as she parked his car in the garage. It read 8:08 AM. That gave her twelve minutes to get to work. Nicole hopped out of Billie's Jag, closing the door and hitting the garage door, closing all in one motion. Nicole ran under the door as it closed, hopped in her Jag, pulling out of the driveway, tires screaming. It was 8:10 AM. Nicole had ten minutes to get to work. She hit La Cienega going eight-five miles per hour.

CHAPTER 8

BILLIE WOKE UP AROUND 9:00 AM. Looking over to Nicole's side of the bed, he noticed she was gone and reached for his phone. "Damn, its 9:00 AM," he said to himself as he got out of bed and headed to the bathroom to take a piss. As he walked through the door, he saw a note taped to it. He grabbed the note, and read it as he walked to the toilet.

> *Daddy, I'm sorry I couldn't be here when you woke up, but I had to go to work. I was going to wake you before I left, but you looked so peaceful and were sleeping so good, so I let you be. I made you some breakfast before I left. It's in the oven waiting for you. I also left the dishes on the stove for you to put in the dishwasher. Yeah, nigga, I cook—you clean. (Lol) I love you and will call*

you on my break. Oh, and just so you know, you
got a bitch walking funny (smile).
Love, yo wife Nicole

Billie laughed as he flushed the toilet. He washed his hands then headed downstairs to get his plate. Once in the kitchen, he began placing the pots and pans Nicole had cooked with inside the dishwasher. When he finished, he opened the fridge, and grabbed a Hawaiian Punch. He kicked the fridge door closed, then grabbed his plate from the oven. It was nice and warm because Nicole had placed the oven on low so his food wouldn't get cold.

"I got a good bitch!" Billie said, as he turned off the oven and ran back up the stairs carrying his plate and Hawaiian Punch.

He sat on the end of the bed, turned the TV to ESPN and was about to start eating when he saw the pink nightie on the floor. Billie sat his plate down then picked up the nightie. Visions of how he had fucked Nicole last night ran through his mind. He remembered how he was thinking about Tasha the whole time he was fucking his girl.

"Damn, that bitch got a fat ass pussy!" Billie said, recalling Tasha bending over in the dressing room, picking up the same nightie he now held in his hand.

Billie had seen Tasha many times in bikinis and knew she had a hell of a body, but he had never seen her completely naked. Even when they were in middle school, Tasha had a body and was fine as fuck. He could remember always liking her, but they were so cool with each other that he didn't want to risk hitting on her and she reject him and then not want to kick it with him or be his friend anymore because he liked her. Billie didn't want to lose her as a friend; he enjoyed her company, as they had a lot in common and she was cool folks, easy to talk to and funny as hell. So he always tried to get at Nicole. As time passed, Tasha was like a part of his life. If you saw Billie, you saw Nicole and Tasha. If you saw Nicole and Tasha, it wouldn't be long before you would see Billie with them. Since the 9th grade, he couldn't remember not being around one of them for a whole day.

He placed the nightie on the bed and picked up his plate, putting a sausage in his mouth, thinking about Tasha's body and what he had seen in that dressing room on Skype. His dick got hard as visions of her ass and hips crossed his mind.

"Fuck," Billie said to himself as he bit into a biscuit.

As he chewed, he remembered the shadow that was in the hallway earlier that afternoon when he and Nicole were in the game room. *Could Tasha have been watching us?* he thought, his dick throbbing as his mind pictured Tasha playing with herself as he fucked Nicole.

"I need to stop doing this to myself," Billie said as he grabbed the remote and turning to Movies On Demand. "I'm letting seeing her nakedness play all kinds of games with my mind." He laughed as he finished eating his food and selected to watch *Face Off*, one of his favorite movies.

* * *

Tasha woke up at 7:30 AM feeling energized, even though she had planned to rest, she was feeling good just staying in bed. Tasha had made herself cum four times last night, which was a record for her. Tasha had never brought herself nor had any man even made her have more than one orgasm. While eating her breakfast, she had received a text from Nicole, Tasha read it with a smile on her face then sent Nicole back a reply after pressing send.

Tasha finished enjoying her meal. She had made up her mind on leaving the games she was playing with Billie alone. She loved Nicole more than anything in this world and knew in her heart that their twenty-eight-year friendship meant more to her than some good dick ever would. Tasha got up from the table, grabbing her plate and placing it in the dishwasher with the skillet she had used to make her breakfast sandwich. She opened the fridge, grabbed the Simply Social orange juice and drunk straight out of the container. Since she lived alone, she could do shit like that! Tasha drunk until her thirst was quenched, before returning the juice to the fridge and heading to her bedroom. It was 8:45 AM. *Damn, what the fuck am I going to do with myself?* Tasha thought as she looked in her closet for what she would wear. When she first got up, Tasha looked out her bedroom window, and it looked a little misty, so she decided to peek outside before choosing her attire for the day.

The sky was clear and the sun was out. *This California weather is a motherfucker*, she thought, closing the blinds going back to her closet. Tasha quickly decided on a lavender and white sheer dress made by Donna Karan New York. The dress was made with a slip, but you could still see through it if the sun were to hit it right. Tasha went into her dresser, grabbed a pair of white thong panties and decided she wouldn't wear a bra. Her breasts were perfectly perky and with the dress, there was no need to wear one. She grabbed a pair of five-inch heels that matched the dress and sat on the bed, sitting the heels down and grabbing her Daily Planner.

Tasha looked at her schedule for Friday and noticed she had a field appointment at 10:30 AM. "Fuck, I forgot all about the Johnson case," Tasha said out loud. She jumped up, making a beeline to the shower. Tasha loved her job. She and Nicole worked for DCFS (Department of Children and Family Services). When they were in high school, they decided they wanted to help kids. They went to college and took Child Psychology, Sociology, Child Care and Child Development. After receiving their BAs, they were hired one month later at the DCFS office in the City of Bellflower. That was six and a half years ago. Tasha and Nicole loved children. The only part that Tasha didn't like about her job was if she felt a home wasn't suitable for a child, she was supposed to take the child away from the parent or parents. Tasha and Nicole hated doing this, and Tasha hated it so much that she found herself working with single moms as much as she could because her mother was a single parent and Tasha remembered how hard it was on her mom when she was growing up. Plus, Tasha knew if she had a child and someone tried to take him or her away from her, she would try to kill their ass or she would die trying to protect hers.

Tasha never took the police with her when she went to a client's house to check on children. She chose to do this because she wanted the families to feel comfortable with her. Also, it built trust and the family would see she really wanted to help them. Only once did Tasha have to call for back up. A scandalous bitch named Mrs. Walker, who lived in the PJs, was selling crack out of her house. Mrs. Walker had three beautiful children, all with different fathers. The oldest at the time was sixteen. Her name was Tiffany and the two youngest were boys: Malcolm was eight and DeJon was six. During her monthly check up, Tasha knocked on the door and she was greeted by a crack head.

"Aw, what up, sexy? You mighty fine, who you looking for?" the crack head asked, smiling showing a mouth void of teeth.

"Ummm, is Mrs. Walker here?" Tasha asked, taking a step back?

"Yeah, sweetie, she in the kitchen cooking. Come on in!"

As Tasha entered the house, the smell of cocaine was so strong she thought she would pass out. As she walked in the kitchen, Mrs. Walker was cooking cocaine in a glass jar, her oldest child Tiffany was sitting at the table in the kitchen, cutting up the dope and the second to the oldest child, Malcolm, was putting it in baggies after his sister passed it to him.

"Mrs. Walker, what the fuck are you doing?" Tasha asked almost yelling.

Shocked and caught off guard, Mrs. Walker dropped the glass jar. "Ooh, my Lord. Ms. Ward, I didn't know you was coming today, how are you?"

"Naw, fuck the small talk! I try to work with you so you can keep your kids and this is the thanks I get? You cooking dope in the house with them here and got them choppin' and baggin' the shit!"

Tasha was heated. Four months ago, she was supposed to have taken Mrs. Walker's kids, but she was giving a single black woman a chance to clean up her act, which is something that is rarely done in the minority communities.

"Well, shit, I gotta do what I gotta do. If you would have called before just popping up, this wouldn't have been going on," Mrs. Walker replied with an attitude.

"You know damn well DCFS shows up unannounced once a month to make sure things are running smooth and the house is a safe environment for the children, and what you're doing right now is way out of line and more than I'm willing to cover up for you. I cannot let you off this time!"

Tiffany pushed herself back from the table and stood up. She was a beautiful young lady. She had long wavy hair, eyes the color of honey and a body most women twice her age would kill for; Tiffany was no more than an inch shorter than Tasha.

"My momma do what she gotta do to take care of us, so if you thinking about taking us, we ain't going nowhere!"

Tasha looked the teenager in her eyes. Tiffany showed no sign of fear.

"I think you need to leave," Tiffany said, now looking Tasha up and down while her mother picked the dope up off the floor.

Is this little bitch sizing me up?!? Tasha wondered, still looking in Tiffany's eyes.

"I'm not going anywhere, young lady, and you need to stay in a child's place. As a matter of fact, Mrs. Walker, I suggest you tell your daughter to go pack for her and her brothers so we can make this as easy as possible," Tasha stated with authority.

Mrs. Walker laughed. "Bitch, please, my kids ain't going nowhere!"

Tasha took a step back, realizing she should have called for backup instead of running her mouth. Just as Tasha was planting her feet from taking her step back, Tiffany rushed her. "Bitch, get up out of here," she yelled, swinging wildly at Tasha.

Tasha dropped her briefcase to the floor.

Eight-year-old Malcolm grabbed Tasha's right leg and bit into it.

"Awe, you little bastard," she yelled as she grabbed Tiffany by the hair and threw her to the floor.

The girl sprung up, this time with her mother at her side.

"AHH HELL NAW," Tasha said as she hit the little boy in the face, making him release her leg. He began crying loudly.

"Ooohh, no you didn't just hit my baby," Mrs. Walker yelled, calling out to the crack head.

Hearing his name, the crack head jumped off the sofa, but was too slow. He grabbed Tasha's shirt, as she was halfway out the door. It ripped in the front, exposing Tasha's bra and breasts.

Tasha was fast, as she and Nicole ran track in high school. She made it to her car within seconds, while people in the projects looked on.

As Tasha opened her car door to get in, she was hit in the back of the head.

"Naw, bitch, you ain't going nowhere," Tiffany stated. Just as she was about to take another swing, Tasha turned around and took off on Tiffany as if she were a grown woman. The little girl could hold her own for her age, but all the Compton came out of Tasha.

"Bitch, you got me fucked up! I was trying to help yo young ass out," Tasha said through clinched teeth. She reached under her car seat, grabbing her .38 Special from its hiding place. Just as Mrs. Walker was coming up on her with a knife in her hand, Tasha cocked the hammer back and aimed the gun at Mrs. Walker's nose. "Bitch, drop the knife or I swear I'll blow yo damn brains out in front of your kids!"

Mrs. Walker dropped the knife and frowned. "I guess I fucked up this time, huh?"

Tasha grabbed her phone out of her pants pocket. "Naw, bitch, you did way more than fuck up."

Tasha hit the #2 button, speed dialing her straight to the local sheriff's department. The operator picked up on the first ring.

"Hi, my name is Tasha Ward with DCFS. I need assistance ASAP at 377 W. 118th Street. I have my service weapon drawn and I am in danger."

"Okay, Ms. Ward, stay on the line with me. Help is on the way!" Within seconds, three police cars were on the scene. That was four years ago.

Tasha laughed as she got out the shower, put lotion on her body and then dressed. Tasha went back into the bathroom to do her hair. She placed it in a wrap and grabbed her white DKNY watch off the bathroom counter, placing it on her arm. It was 9:38 AM and she had more than enough time to get to Ms. Johnson's house on time. Tasha decided to leave so she could stop by Starbucks to get a Carmel Cappuccino. She locked up her house, got in her Lexus, slid Young Money's CD into the stereo system and hit the 105 Freeway.

Tasha made it to Starbucks off La Tijera and La Cienega next to Magic Johnson's TGIF Restaurant at 10:05 AM. She ran inside, got a Carmel Cappuccino, and then hopped back in her car and headed for her 10:30 appointment. Tasha pulled up to Ms. Johnson's house at exactly 10:23 AM. She sat in her car finishing her drink, listening to Escape and Keith Sweat remake of, "Am I Dreaming." Tasha exited her car, headed for Ms. Johnson's front door at 10:29 AM. Once at the door, she rang the doorbell. She waited a few minutes then rang it again. Tasha looked at her watch and it was now 10:33 AM. She took a deep breath, exhaled and was about to leave when she heard the wooden door behind a black iron door opening.

"Hello, how can I help you?" an older black woman asked.

"Good morning, ma'am, my name is Tasha Ward and I work for DCFS." Tasha showed her badge and ID. I have a 10:30 AM appointment with a Zora Johnson, is she here?"

"Oh dear, yes, I forgot all about that, I'm sorry," Ms. Johnson said, unlocking the bar door. "Come right on in." Tasha smiled as she entered the house. "I was asleep; the baby kept me up all night."

"It's okay, ma'am, I understand." Tasha looked around the house. "You have a beautiful home."

"Ooh thank you, sweetie. I've been here for more than thirty-eight years, raised all five of my kids here. This is my youngest daughter's son that you are here about. Go ahead and have a seat."

"Thank you very much," Tasha said, sitting down and opening her briefcase to pull out the folder on the Johnson's case.

"Would you like something to drink, Ms. Ward?"

"Oh no, but thank you for asking."

Ms. Johnson sat down and placed her hand on her lap, as Tasha went through her paperwork.

"Okay, so I see that your daughter, Stacy, had Antwan taken from her, because of neglect and the courts awarded you sole custody," Tasha said, looking at her notes.

"Yeah, sweetie, that's correct. But truth be told, my daughter never neglected her son, it was that sorry motherfucker she had the child by, that's who left the baby in the house alone. I told Stacy he was a sorry son of a bitch," Ms. Johnson stated with anger. "I've raised five kids, all of 'em except one have good jobs and are doing good for themselves. My oldest son is in prison for life for killing the man that raped his sister—my daughter, Kimberly. He was an underwater welder and he would have been doing well himself if that punk nigga wouldn't have fucked with his sister, but I ain't mad at my son. He did what a big brother was supposed to do, he protected his family."

Tasha nodded her head in agreement with Ms. Johnson. She could hear in Ms. Johnson's voice and from what she was sharing that her family had been through a lot of headache and Tasha wanted to be the last person to cause this older black woman, who from what she could see, was doing a damn fine job as a mother and grandma. She didn't need any kind of problems or unnecessary drama.

"Well, Ms. Johnson, I know that you will do all you can do to do right by your grandchild. I don't need to look around nor do we need to go any further with this meeting."

Tasha pulled out some papers from her briefcase that would finalize the custody of the child. "Can you please sign here, here, here and here? You can read them if you'd like."

"Oh no, sweetie, I trust you. I can see you sincerely want to help." Ms. Johnson took the pen that Tasha sat on the table and began signing the papers.

Tasha noticed the baby sleeping in his crib and asked if she could hold him.

"Go ahead, just please don't wake him. That boy's a real piece of work. He wants you to walk around talking to him before he goes to sleep."

Tasha laughed softly as she walked over to the crib, reached in and gently picked up the baby. He smelled so good and was so clean. Tasha held him close to her chest and closed her eyes. The baby felt so right in her arms. Tasha wanted a baby. She wanted to have someone that needed her, no matter what, someone who would love her unconditionally.

Ms. Johnson finished signing the papers and looked over toward Tasha and the baby; a smile graced her face. "I know that look," Ms. Johnson said, snapping Tasha out of her trance.

Tasha looked at Ms. Johnson in puzzlement, while returning the baby to the crib. "What look?" she asked, smiling.

"The look of a woman wanting a baby. You don' have any children do you, sweetie?"

"No, not yet, but I want a family of my own!"

"Well, baby, don't wait too long to start, because the older you are, the more children take out of you."

Tasha laughed. "Yeah, I bet I couldn't imagine chasing after a child in my forties or fifties?"

Ms. Johnson laughed. "Shit, trust me, you don't want to either." They shared a laugh.

"Well, Ms. Johnson, I'm going to leave. You get some rest and it was wonderful meeting you." Tasha handed her a business card with her cell phone number on it. "If you need anything, give me a call."

Ms. Johnson walked her to the door to let her out. She reached for Tasha, giving her a warm hug. "You're a real sweetheart. Don't change for anyone."

Tasha walked to her car feeling something she had never really felt as a woman. She wanted to be a mother. She took a deep breath, started her car and put on her game face. It was almost time for her to meet her best friend at Red Lobster.

Tasha pulled off of Fairview onto La Cienega at 11:07 AM, leaving Ms. Johnson's house. She noticed that she was only three minutes from Nicole's house. Since she had extra time and was in the area, she decided to go by and pick up her bag that she had left in Nicole's car. Tasha made a right instead of the left she was going to make, drove two blocks and turned on Alvern, and pulled into Billie and Nicole's driveway. She turned off her car, opened her glove compartment, grabbed the set of key's Nicole had given her, got out the car and walked to the front door. Tasha stuck her key in the lock, unlocked the door and entered the house.

CHAPTER 9

BILLIE WAS LYING IN BED STILL watching *Face Off*. Although he had watched it a million times, he could never get enough of it. He sat up as a craving for a bag of Act popcorn hit him. Grabbing the remote, he put the DVR on pause, and got out of bed. He thought about calling Nicole to share the news about the new contract, but decided to wait to tell her face-to-face like he had decided when he was first told and she had come home in that nightie making him forget everything. Billie laughed as he grabbed his plate from breakfast and headed down the stairs. He was at the last two steps when Tasha walked out of the den with a Dr. Pepper in her hand, headed for the front door. Tasha had left the front door open because she had intended to grab her bag and leave. Tasha looked at Billie standing on the stairs, naked, dick hanging to his inner thigh.

"I...I...I...came to get my bag," Tasha stuttered, her eyes still glued to Billie's dick. She slowly looked up his body until their eyes met. Her panties were so wet you would have thought they had been dipped in water and she had put them on without ringing them out.

Billie didn't know what to say. Before he could ask Tasha what she was doing there, she had given him the answer. His dick began to stand straight out like a flagpole. He tried to use the plate to hide it.

"Ummmm, did Nicole know you was coming by?" he asked. His dick was now hard as steel.

Tasha backed closer to the front door; her eyes were still locked with his dick. "We...we talked last night. I'ma go now," Tasha said, now standing on the welcome mat.

The sun was coming through the door and Billie could see through Tasha's dress, and he saw that she wasn't wearing a bra and her nipples where hard. His dick began throbbing.

"Alright, cool," Billie said so low that Tasha barely understood him.

Something came over Tasha when she saw the pre-cum on the head of his dick. She kicked the door closed, dropped her bag and walked over to him.

"Tee, what are you doing?" Billie asked, as Tasha took the plate out of his hand, throwing it toward the kitchen and then pushed him down on the stairs. "Tee, I don't think—" Tasha wrapping her mouth around his dick stopped him mid-sentence. He moaned as Tasha started deep throating him, making loud slurping sounds while she massaged his balls with her free hand. Soft moans of pleasure escaped her mouth. She loved the fact that she was finally sucking his dick. Tasha took Billie's dick out of her mouth and ran her tongue down all ten inches of it until she got to his balls. She then began sucking them.

"Oooh, fuck," Billie moaned as Tasha played with his balls in her mouth. "Tasha, we shouldn't be doing this," he moaned."

Tasha pulled his balls out her mouth, making a loud sucking noise and looked him in his eyes. "Shut up and enjoy the moment."

Billie was about to respond when she began deep throating his dick again. His brain went blank as Tasha gave him the best head of his life. Tasha tightened her jaws and throat around his dick as she felt Billie's dick throbbing in her mouth. Billie moaned like a wounded animal as his body shook uncontrollably. His cum shot into her mouth, down her throat and into her stomach. She drained his dick of every ounce of cum before she pulled it out her mouth. Billie couldn't speak. He had never, ever had his dick sucked like that before.

Tasha started placing soft kisses all over his dick. Billie was still trying to catch his breath as Tasha was taking off her panties. Once her panties were off, she stroked his dick until it was completely hard. Tasha hiked her dress up to her waist and lowered herself down on Billie's dick. Her pussy was wet, but it still wasn't ready to receive a dick as big as Billie's was. Her pussy was so tight that she bit her bottom lip and held her breath as the head of Billie's dick entered her.

"Ooh, Lord Jesus," Tasha moaned as the head and ten inches entered her.

Billie was in heaven. Tasha's pussy felt like an extra small glove on a giant's hand. As each inch of his dick slowly entered her, he thought he would lose his mind. After his dick was completely inside her, Tasha slowly moved up and down, letting the walls of her pussy adjust to his dick. They were letting out sounds that neither one of them could explain. Tasha's was from a hunger and lust of wanting someone and something so long and finally getting it and Billie's was of sheer pleasure.

After about the sixth time of Tasha going up and down on his dick, Billie couldn't take it anymore. He unloaded inside of Tasha with a lion like roar. Tasha screamed with pleasure as she felt her own orgasm hit her. They looked in each other's eyes and then hungrily began kissing each other.

Tasha broke the kiss and then rose up off his dick. They moaned as each inch of Billie's dick slowly exited her. Once he was completely out, Tasha got up, fixed her dress and looked at Billie.

"That's what you could have had if you had chosen me, Billie!"

Tasha stated walking toward the door with her usual sway; she grabbed her bags off the floor, walked out the door, closing it behind her leaving Billie lying on the stairs, mouth wide open and dumfounded.

Billie picked himself up off the stairs; he was so confused with the chain of events that had just taken place, he couldn't think straight. He went into the kitchen to clean up the plate that Tasha had thrown and shattered. He grabbed the broom and dustpan and swept up the broken plate, placing it in the trash.

Once done, Billie went upstairs and started getting dressed. He needed to get out the house to get some air and clear his mind. He threw on his clothes, grabbed his phone and headed back downstairs. He passed the spot he had just finished fucking Tasha on, and said out loud, "That bitch got some fire ass pussy.

Damn, a nigga done really fucked up!" He walked out his front door. I'ma have to holla at Tasha!"

He walked out to the driveway, saw his car wasn't there, and smiled. He went back into the house.

Cola is too sweet! he thought as he went through the washroom and into the garage. Once inside his car, Billie went through his contacts, found Tasha's name then hit send. Her phone rang twice before she picked up.

"Hey, you," Tasha answered in a sexy voice.

"Tee, we need to talk about what just happen. I mean, I—"

Tasha cut him off before he could finish. "Look, we can do that, but right now, I am about to meet Nicole for lunch. I'll text you later and we can meet up then."

"Okay, Tee," Billie said, with a sigh of relief. "I guess that's cool. I'll talk to you then."

Tasha giggled. "Why you sound all sad and shit? Nigga, you good! I got you, now I gotta go. I'll be getting back at you for that convo." Tasha hung up on her end.

Billie sat his phone in its holder, and opened the garage, more confused than before.

"I got you," he said out loud, remembering that Tasha used to say those same words when they were younger and it was for sure that she always had his back. Billie smiled as he backed out the driveway and headed for his office. He needed to keep busy until he talked to Tasha about not letting Nicole find out about them.

"Fuck," he said as he turned on Alvern. "I hope I didn't just let my dick get me caught the fuck up!"

*   *   *

Nicole sat patiently inside of Red Lobster, waiting for Tasha. She had been there since 12:15 PM; it was now 12:35 PM. Tasha was late.

Just as Nicole was about to call her, Tasha came rushing through the door. She stood at the entrance. Nicole giggled as she stood up and waved her hand so that her sister and best friend could see her.

Tasha got to the table, sat down and gave a sigh of relief. "Bitch, I'm sorry I'm late. It was a traffic jam on my way here," Tasha lied.

"It's okay," Nicole said, looking across the table at her girl. "I was starting to worry about you. Yo ass ain't never late." They shared a laugh. "Oh, and what's up with that walk?" Nicole asked, noticing the difference in Tasha's walk.

"I hurt my ankle trying to get in here to yo ass," Tasha lied.

"Ahhh, Tee, are you okay?" Nicole asked, genuinely concerned.

"Yeah, I'm fine," Tasha said, starting to feel guilty. "But, fuck my ankle, bitch, I'm hungry. Let's eat!"

They ordered lobster, crab, fried shrimp and seasoned fries. As they ate their food, they talked about everything under the sun. Nicole caught Tasha up on what happen at the office and Tasha told Nicole what happen while she was in the field. While Nicole was talking, Tasha began remembering how good Billie felt inside of her.

"Tasha. Tasha. Tee," Nicole said, while snapping her fingers trying to get Tasha's attention. "Girl, are you okay? You were in a daze with a smile on your face."

"I'm good, Cola, I was just thinking about this show I saw last night and trying to remember the joke that this dude said, so I could share it with you."

"Oh okay, because, bitch, the only time I zone out like that is when I been dicked down," Nicole said, smiling.

They shared a laugh.

Bitch, if you only knew, Tasha thought as they got up to pay their bills and leave. *If you only fuckin' knew.*

Tasha and Nicole made it to the parking lot, hugged, and said their good-byes before going their separate ways, promising to meet up later so they could shop for their outfits for the concert.

As soon as Tasha was at a red light, she called Billie. He picked up on the first ring.

"Billie's Plumbing Service, how can I help you?"

"Hey you, what it do?" Tasha asked in her most seductive and sexy voice.

"Shit, nothing, finishing up at the office. So are you free so we can talk?" Billie asked, wanting to get an understanding between them about what happened and to keep it on the down low.

"Yeah, I got some time. Um, you can meet me at my house in twenty minutes, so we can talk."

"Okay, well it's 1:42 PM. I'll be there at 2:10 PM. Is that cool?"

"Yeah, that's fine, I'll see you then."

"Alright, Tee, bye."

"Bye, Mr. Hall." She giggled as she hung up.

Tasha was already two lights from her house when she placed the call. She pulled in her driveway, opened her garage so Billie could pull his car in and ran in the house. It was 1:15 PM.

Tasha had nineteen minutes. She put on the best of the 90s R&B CD on and poured herself a cup of Remy Martin Red.

Billie pulled into Tasha driveway at 2:10 PM on the dot. He noticed the garage open, so he pulled inside, figuring it was best for his car not to be seen in her driveway in the middle of the day.

Tasha was relaxing, sipping on her second glass of Remy Red when she heard Billie's car pulling into her garage. Tasha walked through her living room to the door that connected her house to the garage. She opened the door just as Billie was pulling completely in. Tasha pressed the small button that was next to the washer, which closed the garage door and waited for Billie to get out of his car.

Billie cut off his Jag engine, and took a deep breath as he opened the door and stepped out the car. He noticed Tasha was standing in the doorway of the entrance to the house, looking at him with her sexy ass hazel eyes, nursing a drink. Billie started walking toward her, trying to figure out the best way to handle this situation they had gotten themselves into.

"Come in," Tasha said, as he reached the door. She stepped aside so Billie could enter.

Tasha smelled like caramel and Billie wanted to take a bite out of her as he stepped in the house. He could hear "Let's Make Love" by Silk playing on the surround sound system throughout the house. *This is about to be harder to deal with than I thought*, he thought, as he walked into the living room to take a seat.

Tasha came over to him with an extra drink in her hand. She handed it to Billie and sat next to him.

"So what is it that's on your mind?" Tasha asked, looking into his eyes.

Billie downed his drink and sat the glass on the end table.

"Tee, look, I don't know that happened with us earlier today, but I—"

Tasha pressed her finger against his lips, silencing him. "Look, Billie, let me go first. I need to get some shit off my chest. Once I'm finished, maybe you'll better understand what happened today, but first let me say this. I didn't know you were home this morning. Now listen." Tasha removed her finger from his lips. "Since the 7th grade, I've liked you. I liked your walk, the way you talk, your attitude, the way you treated women and as well as the way you look. I loved how you would always listen to me and how you took heed to what I would say to you. True, I never tried to get at you nor did I attempt to tell you how I felt, but in ways, I tried to show you in the 8th grade when you started asking about Nicole. I would get too mad, because I used to think to myself, does he not think I'm pretty, or what. Am I fat, etc? So I would try harder to make you notice me by keeping my hair done or wearing tight clothes or low cut dresses even by brushing my ass against you when I would pass by you to sit down next to you in class, but you never said a word, you just brushed me off.

"So when you and Nicole finally started dating, I was heartbroken. I was so fuckin' hurt, but I couldn't be mad at no one but myself for never saying anything about how I felt. So I kept it bottled up. Plus, Nicole is like a sister to me and if I couldn't have you, I would want it to be her. But the other day when I was at your house, I came up stairs to ask Nicole how to use that damn oven and you were making love to her. Well, all those old feelings came back and at that moment, I knew that I should have been the one you was making love to. I should have been the one riding yo dick."

Billie now knew for a fact that he had seen Tasha watching them, because he was starting to think he was crazy.

Tasha took a deep breath. "Well, I ain't going to lie, I got turned on, so I stayed and enjoyed the show, the whole time imagining it was me you was fucking. After I left your house, I couldn't get you out my mind' all this stuff we—well I'm telling you now started playing back in my head. So when you called for Nicole when we was at the mall together on my phone, I acted like I didn't know it wasn't hung up and set it on the seat so you could see me. I knew it was wrong, but I wanted to get you back for not liking me. I wanted to put myself on your mind like you are on mine." A tear fell from Tasha's eye. Billie wiped it away.

"Tee, don't cry, it wasn't like that fo' real, fo' real." He grabbed her hand. "Tee, I liked you too in junior high school, but I was a little shy. I thought you was so fine and way too cool to want to be with me. Shit, you don't even know how much my boys envied me, just from seeing me sitting and talking to you in class or eating lunch with you, walking with you to our classes. I felt special just doing that. I didn't want to run you off by trying to get at you, so I just started asking about Nicole, but know that you've always been fine as fuck to me. Always!"

That brought a smile to Tasha's face. She punched him in the arm.

"Nigga, you could have at least tried and risk losing out on just being around me every day. Fuck that."

"I knew I didn't have no game back then and I didn't want to chance it."

They both shared a laugh.

Billie continued. "I never really expected Nicole to give me a chance, it was just for conversation. I would bring her up, because I was at a loss for words, or one of my boys would ask, 'Ay, what up with your girlfriend?' Shit, honestly all my boys thought I was with you. The day you told me Nicole said she'd go out with me; I was mind blown and from there is how we got here. Most of my boys, even to this day, think I dated you first then got with Nicole. Once I got with Nicole, I knew there would never be a chance on Earth that I would get you, because of how close y'all are. So I stayed focused on her. Plus, it was a bonus, because I still got to be around you."

Tasha remembered how she would always talk about how cool and down to earth Billie was when she and Nicole were together. She remembered telling her how he listened and liked all the same movies and music they both liked.

"Shit, I'm the reason she gave you a chance," Tasha admitted. "I used to talk about you to her, ninety-going-north. I used to tell her how you asked about her every day; how you're funny, cool, down to earth, fine and don't be trying to spit game at me until finally she told me to tell you she'd go out with you. Oh, my God, I did this to myself!" Tasha covered her mouth.

"Yeah, because that day at lunch, when we was eating together and you told me Nicole would go out with me that was the last thing I was expecting."

They sat quietly for a moment, lost in thought. Tasha was the first to speak up.

"Okay, so we now know what happened then. Now what are we gonna do about what we've done now? I don't want to hurt

Nicole, she's been in my life all my life," Tasha said, looking at Billie.

"Well, we can act like it never happened," Billie replied, and just like when they were in middle school, he waited on the edge of his seat for her to respond.

Tasha started laughing.

"What's funny, did I miss something?" Billie asked, looking puzzled.

"You still sit on the end of the chair when you're waiting to hear what I'm going to say. I've always thought that was so cute!"

It had been years since middle school that someone had paid attention to her every word and Billie was that someone then and still was that someone now.

Tasha lowered her head. "Maybe that would be best," she said so low that Billie wasn't sure if he heard her correctly.

He put his index finger on her chin pushing her head up so that he could look into her eyes. "What did you say, Tee?" He looked into her hazel eyes.

"I…I said, maybe—"

Billie cut her response short by kissing her lips. Tasha responded to the kiss as if it was as normal as breathing. Their tongues danced as their hands hungrily ran over each other's body. They had shared feelings for each other that they had locked away. Tasha broke her silence as one of Billie's fingers slide inside of her. The sensation took her breath away. Tasha looked into Billie's eyes.

"Are you sure you want to do this?" she asked, as Billie pumped his index finger in and out of her pussy, while his thumb played with her clit.

Billie lightly kissed her lips. "Shut up and enjoy the moment."

Tasha giggled. "You're such a copycat," she said, and then moaned Billie's name as he pushed his index finger deeper inside of her wet pussy. Tasha unbuttoned his jeans then pulled his boxers and pants down to his knees. Billie kicked off his shoes, then used his left foot to kick his pants and boxers off as well. His dick was standing straight as a pole. Tasha grabbed it and began sucking the head and playing with it with her tongue. Billie began to throb in her hand. Tasha rolled her tongue around the head once more and then took all ten inches of his dick completely in her mouth. She began deep throating his dick, causing Billie to moan her name. Tasha loved the way her name sounded coming out of his mouth. She tightened her jaws and throat on his dick, moaning as loud slurping sounds echoed over the music. Billie grabbed her waist, pulling her body toward him so that her pussy was in his face. Tasha kept to her duties as he positioned her so he could eat her pussy. Tasha almost chocked when she felt his warm mouth and tongue sucking and licking on her clit. She had to pull his dick out her mouth so her moans of pleasure could escape her throat.

"Ooh, Billie…yes, nigga eat this pussy…damn nigga…ooh shit," Tasha moaned, while stroking his dick. Her body began jerking as she felt a mind-blowing orgasm about to be released from deep within.

Billie ran his tongue around Tasha's asshole, and just as she screamed, she was cumming. He stuck his tongue inside her pussy and began sucking as Tasha went limp having one of the best orgasm of her life. She came hard and lost control of her whole body. Billie slowly adjusted her so that she was now lying on the sofa. Tasha was still holding on to his dick as if it was a prize that she was not going to lose.

"Tasha, baby!"

She opened her eyes, hearing him call her name.

"Let's go so I can make love to you."

Tasha looked deep in his eyes. "Billie, please," she moaned, as she let go of his dick. "Make love to me!"

Billie picked her up and kissed her lips as he walked her into her bedroom. Tasha held on tightly, never wanting to let him go.

He laid her on the bed and climbed on top of her, and then he started sucking on her breast.

"Ooh God, yes," Tasha moaned as Billie ran his tongue over her nipples. She reached between his legs, grabbing his dick and guiding it inside of her wet tight pussy. Billie found his way to her lips and then began kissing as he tried to work his dick into her. Tasha's pussy was just as tight as before. She dug her nails into his back as the head of his dick entered her. She bit down on Billie's shoulders and wrapped her legs tightly around his lower back as she felt him easing into her inch by inch. They both were moaning loudly. This was the tightest pussy besides Nicole that Billie had ever had and for Tasha, by far, the biggest dick she'd ever had inside her.

"Ooh, B-i-l-l-i-e," Tasha moaned as all ten inches of his dick was now inside of her. She moaned, screamed and yelled his name out as they made love while Black Street's "Before I Let Go" played softly throughout the house.

Billie began speeding up, feeling himself about to cum. Tasha tightened her legs around him as she worked her hips, wanting all of his cum to be inside of her. Billie moaned her name out loudly as he gave her a deep thrust which made him lose his breath while his cum shot inside her.

"Ooh, Billie, yes cum for me…cum, baby, yes," Tasha moaned as he lay on top of her catching his breath. She held him close to her. His dick was still deep inside her. She tightened her walls on his dick and placed soft kisses on his chest, neck and face.

"Damn, you got some good ass pussy," he moaned, as he pulled his dick out of her and lay next to her.

Tasha stole another kiss. "And you got some bomb ass dick." Tasha snuggled up under him, feeling safe in his arms.

Billie's last words were, "What are we getting ourselves into," as they drifted off to sleep.

CHAPTER 10

IT WAS 4:45 PM. NICOLE WOULD be getting off work in fifteen minutes. She had been blowing her girl, Tasha's, phone up for the last hour, but she wasn't picking up. It had Nicole a little concerned, because that was not like Tasha to not pick up her phone. Nicole figured Tasha must have had another appointment and couldn't pick up. Nicole shut off her computer and started cleaning up her desk. It was Friday, and she couldn't wait to start her weekend. She decided to call Billie to see what was up with him. She called his cell phone; the voice mail picked up on the fifth ring. She left a message, and then called his office. His secretary picked up on the third ring.

"Billie's Plumbing Service, how can I help you?"

"Hey, Mo, it's me, Nicole. Is my man around?"

"Oh, hey girl. Nah, he left for an appointment about two hours or so ago. I don't think he's coming back in, but if he does, I'll let him know you called."

"Nah, girl, that's okay. I'll just text him, but thank you anyway," Nicole replied.

"No problem, boss lady, anytime. Have a blessed day."

"You, too," Nicole said, and then hung up the phone.

She still had eight minutes before she could clock out, so she picked up her cell phone and purse and headed to the elevator. She sent Tasha a text telling her she'd meet her at her house at 6:00 PM and sent Billie a text letting him know she'd be at Tasha's, and that she loved him and would see him at home a little later. She got on the elevator, headed to the first floor so she could clock out and start her weekend.

* * *

Tasha was awakened by her cell phone; it kept going off. She gently pulled away from up under Billie's arm so she wouldn't wake him and grabbed her phone off the charger. She had eighteen messages, thirty-eight missed calls and five new texts. She looked at the time. It was 5:15 PM. Tasha decided to let Billie sleep a little longer in her bed until she read one of Nicole's texts.

"Ooh shit," she said as she dropped her phone on the night-stand, and then reached over and shook Billie.

Billie sat up, rubbing his eyes. "What's wrong, Tee?" he asked in a sleepy voice, his dick was standing straight up, hard as steel.

At the sight of it, Tasha's pussy began to throb and get wet. She licked her lips wanting to put his dick back in her mouth. She lost her train of thought for a moment, thinking about how good his dick tasted, when her phone went off again with a new text, snapping her back to reality.

"You need to get up. Nicole texted me, letting me know she is on her way over here. She said she will be here by 6:00 PM."

That snapped Billie wide-awake. "What time is it?" he asked, springing up out of bed, looking for his clothes.

Tasha laid there watching him, as he looked around for his clothes, naked. She began rubbing her clit enjoying the view. It was now 5:24 PM. Tasha moaned which made Billie look over his shoulder.

"Tee, what are—" He stopped in mid-sentence seeing her playing with herself. "Tasha we can't, Cola will be here in less than forty-five minutes. It's cutting it too close," he moaned; his eyes glued to Tasha's hand movement. "Damn, bitch, you fuck-ing with a nigga's head."

Tasha giggled, stopped playing with herself and started crawling to the edge of the bed where Billie was standing.

"We got time for a quickie, don't we?" Tasha asked, seductively.

Billie looked at her phone. It was now 5:31 PM. "Tee, we would be cutting it too—"

Tasha started sucking his dick, which made him forget all about the time and his train of thought.

"Damn, Tee," he moaned as she sucked his dick, stroking him slowly while massaging his balls. She slowly pulled his dick out her mouth and looked up at him, still stroking him with one hand while massaging his balls with the other.

"Promise me I'ma see you again and soon!"

"Ooh, Tasha, damn. I can't."

Tasha deep throated his dick and sucked on the head for a few seconds before pulling his dick out her mouth. Billie moaned her name as she played with the head of his dick with her tongue.

"Promise me!" she demanded.

"Ooh Tee, babe, I promise.

Tasha kissed the head of his dick then hopped off the bed. "That's all I wanted," she stated, and then kissed him on the lips as he stood there dumbfounded, dick standing straight out like a flagpole.

"You better hurry up, it's 5:39 PM," Tasha said, bending over in front of him giving him a view of her heart-shaped ass and pussy from the back as she grabbed her dress.

"You a cold bitch," Billie said, pulling his drawers and pants up, and then smacking her on the ass.

Tasha stood up, turned around then laughed. "I can be when needed. I'm not finished with you yet, and until we decide how we're going to keep this shit under wraps, we need to make time for each other, so we can talk."

Billie threw his shirt on and then laughed. "Yeah, okay just talk," he said, sarcastically.

"Boy, get yo ass out of here before we both be dead, it's 5:49 PM."

Billie grabbed his keys then went into the garage. Tasha followed him naked, opening the garage door so he could pull out. As he backed his Jag out her garage, they held eye contact with each other until the door closed.

As Billie was hitting the corner, he laughed. "That's one cold ass bitch!" He turned on Atlantic then hopped on the 91 Freeway headed for his office, trying to figure out how he let himself get caught up in Tasha's web.

Tasha took a quick shower, put on some jeans and a wife-beater not bothering to put on panties or a bra, got herself a glass of Remy Red then sat on the sofa, sipping her drink and think-ing about what she was doing and had done. Tasha realized that she didn't feel bad at all. Yeah, she didn't want to hurt her best friend, but at the same time, she didn't want to neglect herself anymore. She loved Nicole like a sister, but she also loved her-self and felt she deserved to have her wants fulfilled, too.

"I'm being selfish," she said out loud, as she finished the last of her drink. Tasha got up and poured herself another drink. "I'll break it off if she and Billie decide to get married, or if he really wants to, but until then, what she doesn't know won't hurt her."

Tasha picked up her cell phone and looked at the time. It was 6:00 PM. Nicole's phone rung twice on her car's blue tooth system before she hit answer on her steering wheel.

"Hello," she answered, while weaving around a truck that had on its hazard lights.

"Cola, what's good?"

"Shit, nothing bitch, I been trying to call you, but yo phone was just ringing. What's up?"

"Ooh shit, girl, I got caught up. That lady, Ms. Johnson, called me and asked me for a copy of the papers that I had her sign. I told her okay and took her a set. Once I got there, we got to talking about the baby and her kids. I had left my phone in the car thinking I was only going to be a minute; it ended up being hours," Tasha lied, amazed at how easy it was for her to lie to her best friend.

"Girl, I knew it had to do with work, because that's the only time you don't pick up my calls. Did you get my text?" Nicole asked, as she turned on Tasha's block.

"Yeah bitch, you said you'd be here by 6:00 PM, its 6:05. Where you at? Yo ass is late."

Nicole laughed, and then honked her horn. "I'm in your driveway, bitch. Open the front door."

As Tasha stood in the front door watching her best friend walk up her walkway smiling at her, all the guilt that she wasn't feeling hit her so hard it almost made her knees buckle. Twenty-eight years of friendship could be ripped to shreds over a few hours of pleasure. Tasha decided right then that this would have to stay in the closet, because there was no way she would ever let her best friend, her sister, the one person she knew she could count on and trust know that she had seduced her man.

Nicole walked through the door and gave Tasha a hug. "What it do, bitch? I missed yo ass today?"

Tasha snapped out her dazed as she returned the hug and closed the door. "Shit! You ain›t the only one; I missed you, too."

"So what's on the agenda?" Nicole walked over to the sofa in the living room and sat down.

"Shit, I'm game for whatever. You know we still ain't got our clothes for that concert. So let's shoot to the mall. While we at the mall we can get something to eat, too, because a bitch is starving."

"That sounds good to me. I'ma text Billie, see if he's hungry. If so, I'll pick him up something on the way home. He might want to eat the leftovers from last night, but you never know with him."

"Let's do this," Tasha said, downing the last of her drink, "but you going to have to drive, I done had one drink too many."

Nicole jumped off the sofa. "Bitch, I'll drive, but I'ma have me a glass of Remy before we go. I need to relax." They shared a laugh.

"Well, I'ma go get my shoes and a coat." Tasha started walking toward her bedroom. "Well you know where everything is at."

"Nicole was already walking into the kitchen. "Bitch, I'm two steps ahead of you."

Tasha went in her room, put on her all white Air Force Ones, and then grabbed her white leather Pelle Pelle jacket. She came out her room just as Nicole was finishing her glass of Remy.

"Bitch, that's a big ass cup, that's more like, two glasses than one," Tasha said, giggling as Nicole finished it off.

"So what, who you be, the Po Po?"

They laughed.

"Nah, bitch, I'm the bitch that's gonna post yo bail when you fail the breathalyzer."

They shared another laugh.

"Come on, bitch, let's get to the mall before I say fuck it and we order a pizza, get drunk and fall asleep talking about shit we used to do."

Tasha new damn well she didn't want too much more to drink with Nicole there because when she got drunk, she told the truth, confessed and some more shit.

"Yeah, bitch, lets exit stage left, because me getting drunk right now with yo ass might have me regretting some shit I say in the morning when I wake up."

Nicole laughed as she walked out the door. "Yeah, 'cause you know I'ma clown yo ass about whatever you start confessing when we sober up." Nicole pulled out her cell phone to call Billie as Tasha locked her front door, laughing but thinking to herself, *Nah, bitch, this time you wouldn't be clowning me, you'd be trying to kill me!*

They started toward the car just as Billie picked up his phone on the third ring. Billie was sitting in his office going over payroll with his secretary, Monica, when his cell phone rung. He didn't bother to look at the caller ID, he just answered on the third ring.

"Billie's Plumbing and Service, this is Billie, how may I help you?"

"Hi, my name is Ms. White," Nicole said, trying to keep herself from laughing. "I have some pipes that need some special attention. Do you think you're the man for the job?"

Billie laughed. "Well, ma'am, I am very good at what I do. When would you like me to come by and check them out?"

"Shit, right now, my pussy is hungry for some more of that Rod." They started laughing.

"Hey, babe. What's good?"

"Nothing, Daddy, just missing you. What you doing?"

"Shit, going over the payroll. I'll be done in an hour or so then I'll be heading home."

"Oh okay, well I'm going to the mall with Tee. We going to get our outfits for the Trey Songz concert since I had to stop shopping yesterday to get home, because of an issue that needed to be addressed," Nicole said, while giggling, remembering how he had put it down on her. Nicole was hoping she could get served like that again tonight; her pussy got wet with the thought. I was calling to ask you if you wanted me to pick you up something to eat on my way home," she said, as she backed out of Tasha's driveway.

"Yeah, can you stop by Woody's Bar-B-Q and pick me up a rib dinner? I got a taste for some Bar-B-Q."

"Sure, Daddy, and I'ma get some extra sauce so you can lick some off me later," Nicole said in a seductive voice.

"Hmm, that sounds like a plan. Oh and I got something to share with you, too, it's really good news. I'll tell you when you get home."

"Okay, Daddy, it's a date now. Go ahead and finish your pay-roll. I love you and will see you in a little while."

"Alright, love you, too. Oh, and don't forget that extra sauce," Billie said, with a devilish smile on his face, and then hung up before she could respond.

Nicole got on the 91 Freeway West with a big smile on her face. Tasha sat in the passenger seat playing Angry Birds in Space on her Galaxy III, listening to Nicole talking to Billie. She didn't understand why, but she was getting jealous and just as angry as the birds on the game she was playing at the conver-sation she was overhearing. Tasha damn near broke her phone in half hearing Nicole talk about him licking some Bar-B-Q sauce off her. Tasha kept playing the game as they got on the 91 headed to the Lakewood Mall. In her mind, she knew that Billie was Nicole's man, but in her heart, she felt he had always been hers.

Tasha didn't want to hurt Nicole, but she realized that it was going to be a lot harder to leave Billie alone than she thought it would be. She looked over at Nicole with envy as she hung up the phone with a Kool-Aid smile on her face. Tasha found herself mad as a mother bear stripped of her cubs, because it wasn't her picking up his food from Woody's with the extra sauce.

Billie had been keeping busy since he left Tasha's house. He had to keep his mind on something because if he didn't it would have been on Tasha. He felt guilty as fuck of fucking his girl's best friend. He wasn't an angel, but he never played that close to home and he would never, in a million years, shit in his own back yard, but today he broke all the rules...not only once, but also twice. He had only meant to confront Tasha about what they had done earlier in hopes that they could let bygones be bygones and forget it ever happened, but things didn't work as he planned. Feelings that they both had locked away deep inside themselves came out and they ended up getting caught up even deeper than they already were and to make matters worse, Tasha had some fire ass head, with some bomb ass pussy.

"Damn," Billie said out loud, slamming his fist on the desk scaring his secretary, Monica. His dick had gotten hard from the thought of Tasha. He stood up to take a walk and Monica noticed the bulge in his pants and licked her lips, wanting to perform the part of her job that she loved the best.

"Would you like me to help you get rid of some of that stress, boss?" Monica asked, walking over to him.

Billie sat back down in his chair and unzipped his pants. He pulled out his dick, still thinking of Tasha.

"Yeah, do you," he said, as Monica grabbed his dick slowly stroking it. Monica got on her knees and began performing one of her duties that she loved doing for Billie—sucking his dick.

Nicole and Tasha made it to the mall at 7:00 PM. They had found their outfits with shoes to match. Nicole chose a one piece, tight fitting leather Louis Vuitton cat suit, a gold Louis Vuitton belt and some seven-inch Louis Vuitton heels to match, which hit her for $2,889.78. Tasha picked the same outfit, but hers was a two-piece, and it cost her $3,159.37. Both outfits showed every curve on their bodies. They decided to take a break for a bite to eat before picking out their purses to match their outfits. They walked to the food court, both agreeing to eat at Panda Express. They ordered their food and sat down to eat, excited about the concert.

"So, bitch, how you wanna meet up the day of concert?" Tasha asked, putting some Orange Chicken in her mouth. "Y'all gonna pick me up at my house, or do you want me to meet y'all at home?" Either way, I'm game."

Nicole was chewing on some Hot and Spicy Chicken. "I was thinking about that while we was picking out our outfits. I think it'd be better if you just spend the night at our house the night before or come early that morning. Shit, we got a guest room and yo ass is family, so you know the business. That way we ain't gotta be rushing, we can get up and eat breakfast. The concert starts at 1:00 PM, and ends at 3:30 AM, plus we got backstage passes. I want to see everybody that's going to per-form. Girl, Drake, Lil' Wayne, Rick Ross and that nigga Two Chains supposed to be there, so we gotta get there at least an hour early."

Tasha's mind was on being in the same house with Billie overnight. She was playing with her food, lost in thought.

"Tee," Nicole said, snapping Tasha out of her trance. "You listening to me, bitch?"

"Oh yeah, I just went on one thinking about Drake's fine ass," she lied. "Shit, well since we gotta get up early, spending the night will be the best bet," Tasha agreed, now picking at her Shrimp Fried Rice.

Nicole smiled. "It'll be like old times, bitch. We can make some popcorn, watch movies and joke all night. OMG, bitch, it's on Saturday night!"

They shared a laugh.

"Yeah, it's going to be a blast," Tasha stated, as she put a forkful of Shrimp Fried Rice in her mouth, wondering how she was going to control herself being that close to Billie. Tasha had never pondered on this before, because until now it had never been an issue. Now it was.

They finished their food and headed back to the Louis Vuitton store to find the purses to match their outfit.

Nicole and Tasha left the mall at 8:45 PM. Nicole was in a hurry, she wanted to make sure she got Billie's food before Woody's closed. She wasn't sure if it closed at 9:30 PM or 10:00 PM. Either way, Nicole wanted to make sure she got there before they closed.

"Tee, can you look up the number for me then place a phone order so the food will be ready when I get there and I won't have to wait?"

Tasha pulled her Internet up on her phone. "No problem, sis," she responded.

As the number came up, she scrolled down past the address, and then pressed send as they were getting on 91 East.

"Woody's Bar-B-Q, how can I help you?" an elderly black woman answered on the second ring with a southern swagger.

"Hi, I would like to place a pick up order," Tasha said, while placing the phone on speaker so Nicole could place the order herself.

"Oh, sweet heart, you just on time we stop taking phone orders at 9:00 PM. What would you like?"

Nicole thanked God as she looked at her watch; it was 8:57 PM. "Okay, can we have a Rib dinner with Potato Salad, Mac and Cheese, Greens with a side of Cornbread?"

"Would you like a rack or a half a rack?" The elderly woman asked.

"A half rack, please," Nicole replied as she exited the 91 East on Atlantic.

"Would you like something to drink with that?"

Nicole kept the fridge stocked with Billie's favorite drinks, so there was no need to buy one.

"No, ma'am, that'll be all."

"Okay, sweetie, that'll be $14.75. Your order will be ready in fifteen minutes. We close at 9:30 PM, please try to get here before then. What's your name and what's the number you can be reached at?"

Nicole gave her name and number as she pulled into Tasha's driveway.

"Okay, ma'am. Thank you for your order. Have a blessed night."

"You, too," Nicole replied, before Tasha hung up the phone.

They gave each other a quick hug, said their good-byes and Tasha grabbed her bags out of the backseat. Nicole pulled out the driveway and headed back to the freeway. It was 9:08 PM. She honked her horn two times, waving out the window, as she hit the corner headed to Woody's.

CHAPTER 11

TASHA OPENED THE FRONT DOOR, DROPPING the bags as she walked in. She closed the door, locked the dead bolt and kicked off her shoes. She went into the kitchen, pulled out the Remy and poured a tall cup. Tasha walked into the living room, drink in hand, and fell onto the sofa. A little of her drink splashed on her hand, which she gladly licked off with her tongue. Tasha downed half the cup and sat the glass down on the end table. She grabbed the remote, turning on the seventy-two-inch 3D HD Sony flat screen TV. The TV watched her as she got lost in thought about her and Billie's sexual encounter. She grabbed the cup off the end table, finishing the other half of her drink. Tasha then got up, went back to the kitchen for a refill. She grabbed her phone from the table by the door where she had left it with her bags and went back to the sofa. Tasha went through her contacts, downed half the drink, found the number she was looking for and then hit send as she downed the other half of the cup of Remy.

Billie was lying in bed watching UFC fighting when his phone rang. He grabbed the remote, hit mute and answered his phone. "Hello!"

"What's up, Billie?" Tasha said, seductively rolling his name off her tongue. Tasha was feeling herself. She was buzzing and wanted to express her feelings. Billie was caught off guard with the call. He jumped out the bed, ran to the window and looked out to make sure Nicole wasn't pulling up yet. Then he ran down the stairs, checking the house, making sure she wasn't somewhere listening in on his call.

"Uh, Tee, what's up?" he whispered.

"You nigga, that's what's up," Tasha replied with attitude, feeling her pussy getting wet from hearing his voice. "I don't know how we gonna deal with this, but I want you to know that right now, I'm not leaving you alone. So I don't know what you gonna have to do to make this shit work, but for now you got two bitches and we gonna have to figure out how, when and where you going to fit me in, but you're going to fit me in because I'm not going to come up short. We going to keep this on the down low; no ifs, ands, or buts. I need to get you out my system, but until I do, yo ass gonna deal with me, okay Billie?" Tasha asked, but really didn't care for an answer. Her mind was made up and with the help of her good friend, Remy Martin, she was bold enough to speak it.

"Look Tasha, you been on my mind, too, alright? But I think this shit gonna get ugly. We shittin' in our own back yard, feel me?"

"As long as we clean it up, the shit won't get stepped in," Tasha responded. "So nigga, tighten yo game up, because you got a bench warmer that can more than do the job as a starter when needed."

Billie laughed. "Tee, you drunk, huh?" he asked knowing that she was.

"Boo, it don't matter, because I know what I'm saying right now and I know what I want and for now it's you. It's been you since the seventh grade!"

"Okay Tee, you got that," Billie replied, not wanting to hurt her feelings nor piss her off. "We can explore this, but we gotta stay on point." Billie looked out the window. "As a matter of fact, I gotta go before Nicole pulls up. We will talk tomorrow, alright?"

"Yeah, okay. You make sure you tighten yo game up, nigga!"

Tasha hung up before letting him respond. Billie looked at his phone with a smirk, wandering what he had gotten himself into as he heard Nicole opening the garage. Nicole opened the front door. Before she could make it completely in the house, Billie was at her aide grabbing most of the bags she was holding, giving her a kiss on the lips.

"Hey, Cola," he greeted as he ended the kiss and took off up the stairs with the bags.

"Hey, Daddy," Nicole said, smiling as he took the stairs two at a time going up, and then coming back down the same way, grabbing four of the last five bags. He did a repeat of running the last of the bags up the stairs as Nicole giggled and took the one bag he left her with into the kitchen, which was the food from Woody's.

Just as she was sitting the food on the counter, Billie came up behind her putting both hands on the counter top, locking her in place. He began kissing her on the neck.

Nicole moaned, "Emm, so I see you missed me," as she slowly grinded her ass in a circle on his dick.

Billie moved from her neck to her ear, nibbling softly then whispered, "Naw, I thought you was a rib; a nigga starving!"

Nicole spun around so that she was now facing him. She laughed. "What the fuck ever, nigga!" He joined in the laughter. "Now go sit down so I can make your plate, Mr. I'm Starving!"

Billie kissed her again. "Naw, Cola, you sit down. You been at the mall on yo feet shopping all evening and was sweet enough to stop and pick me up something to eat. The least I can do is make my own plate."

Nicole wrapped her arms around Billie's neck and kissed him. "You're such a sweetheart."

They began kissing. Nicole could feel Billie's dick getting hard threw his jeans. She reached down, grabbed his dick and broke the kiss. "You need to eat up all your food, Daddy," she said in a seductive tone. "Because you gonna need all your energy.

Nicole slipped from underneath his arms and giggled as he smacked her on her ass. Nicole headed toward the stairs. "I'ma go get cleaned up," she stated, looking over her shoulder. "Enjoy your meal. Oh, I got that extra sauce you asked for," she said, now smiling. "Can't wait to see what you do with it."

Nicole walked up the stairs, swaying her ass and hips more than usual. Billie took a rib out the bag, enjoying not only the view of her perfectly round ass, but also the food from his favorite Bar-B-Q place.

"It's on," he said, as he chewed a mouthful of tender beef. He turned around to the bag and saw the food containers of extra

Bar-B-Q sauce. A devilish smile crossed his face. "Ooh, it's so, so on!"

Billie started on another rib, thinking of what parts of Nicole's body he was going to start on first with the extra sauce.

Nicole took a shower, moisturized with watermelon-scented lotion and was now lying in bed wearing boy shorts and a wife-beater with no bra, enjoying Housewives of Atlanta on TV when Billie walked into the room, looking full with one of his hands behind his back and a Kool-Aid smile on his face.

Nicole watched him suspiciously. "Daddy, why do you have that look on your face, and what's behind your back?"

Billie walked to the foot of the bed. "Wouldn't you like to know," he mocked, smiling.

Nicole, noticing the bulge in his pants, licked her lips. Billie pulled a container of the extra sauce from behind his back, just as Nicole reached for his zipper.

"Look what I got," he said, as Nicole unzipped his pants, pulled out his dick and began stroking it with one hand, massaging his balls with the other.

Billie let out a moan of pleasure as her tongue rolled around the head of his dick and slowly entered her mouth. He placed his hand on the back of her head as she sucked his dick. They locked eyes as Nicole began deep throating his dick, making loud slurping noises. Billie's knees buckled when Nicole pulled his dick out her mouth, ran her tongue from the tip of his dick to the end and started deep throating him again. Billie closed his eyes, visions of Tasha giving him head ran through his mind. He tightened the grip on Nicole's neck as he started to shake. His body convulsed and he moaned Nicole's name as he came down her throat.

Nicole kept her jaws and throat as tight as she could around his dick until she felt she had drained him of every drop of cum. She pulled his dick out of her mouth, stilling holding on to it. She began placing soft kisses on the head and stroking his dick tenderly. Nicole unbuttoned his pants with her teeth while still stroking Billie's dick. His pants slowly fell to his knees. Nicole, not missing a beat, let go of his dick and pulled down his boxers. She started sucking on his balls as she grabbed his dick so she could stroke it again.

Billie's dick grew in her hand as she ran her tongue up the shaft of his dick to the head then kissed it. It was now at its full length. Nicole smiled at her handy work then kissed the head.

"Daddy, you ready to beat this pussy up?" she asked seductively, then put the head of Billie's dick in her mouth rolling her tongue around it a few times before pulling it out. Billie opened his eyes and looked into Nicole's. The look on his face said it all; he stepped out his boxers and pants, kicking them across the room. He hungrily pulled off Nicole's shorts and then her wife-beater; her nipples were so hard they looked as if they were pointing. Billie ran his tongue around her left nipple, and then placed it inside his mouth. A moan escaped Nicole's lips as he sucked her nipple like a newborn baby.

"Ooh, Daddy, don't stop please," Nicole begged, as she felt his tongue run down her stomach to her belly button and then to her inner thighs.

Billie spread Nicole's pussy lips and began sucking, licking and running his tongue in circles around her clit and then jabbing it in and out of her pussy.

Nicole moaned uncontrollably as she grabbed Billie's head while he ate her pussy. She locked her legs around his neck and shoulders and began thrusting her hips, fucking his face. Her whole body started shaking violently as she lost control of herself and began screaming out Billie's name as she had a mind-blowing orgasm so intense that she completely blacked out for a few seconds. Her pussy was throbbing and so wet that it looked like someone had poured a gallon of water between her legs and then on Billie's face.

Billie stood up then climbed on top of her. Nicole was still in a daze, her eyes were open, but she was mentally in another world. When she felt Billie's dick entering her, she snapped back to reality and dug her nails into his back as her pussy swallowed his dick.

"Ooh, Daddy, ooh my God," Nicole moaned as he thrust hard into her letting out a moan of his own.

Billie placed her legs on his shoulders grabbed her hips and began pounding Nicole's pussy. Before each inward stroke, Billie would pull his full ten inches out of her; the lips of Nicole's pussy seemed to beg his dick not to completely exit her. Nicole's pussy lips clutched the head of his dick not letting all of the ten inches escape. Billie tightened his grip on her hips, ramming himself in and out of her with all his strength.

Nicole moaned so loud it was almost a scream.

"Bitch, this is what you want?" Billie asked, still ramming into her with all his force.

"Oooh God, Yyyesss! Ooooooh, Daddy, yessss!" Nicole's response was a shallow raspy moan. Her body began to shake and her eyes rolled back in her head as she had a gut wrenching orgasm, which took her breath away.

Billie, feeling himself about to cum, continued to ram himself in and out of Nicole. Then, with a lion like roar, he released his seed inside her. He lowered her legs off his shoulders. Nicole was asleep before her legs hit the bed. Billie closed his eyes not understanding what had just come over him. His last thought before he drifted off to sleep was that he didn't get to use the extra sauce.

CHAPTER 12

TASHA WOKE UP WITH A SERIOUS hangover, after drinking a fifth of Remy and three shots of Parton before finding her way to her bedroom. Masturbating, thinking about Billie fucking her, and bringing on two gut-wrenching, breathtaking orgasms, she fell asleep naked with her legs wide open as if Billie were between them. Tasha looked at the time on her DVR. It was 11:00 AM. She hopped up and headed to the bathroom to take a cold shower. As she walked by her mirrored-closet door, she looked at her reflection.

"This nigga got you all twisted in the head and he's your best friend's man," she said to her mirror image.

Tasha walked into her bathroom, turned on the shower, and stepped in, hoping a cold shower would bring her back to herself.

Tasha took a long shower, taking her time washing every part of her body with Banana Strawberry Shower Gel. After she was satisfied, she stepped out the shower, dried off, and moisturized with lotion. Tasha looked at the DVR once again for the time: 12:28 PM. Her cell phone rung as she was getting a pair of panties with a matching bra out of her dresser drawer. She tossed the panties and bra on the bed, looked to see whom was calling, and then touched the screen to answer the call.

"What it do, bitch?" Nicole said, as soon as the call was connected.

Tasha placed the phone on speaker so she could finish getting dressed and be hands free.

"Shit nothing, just got out the shower; I'm getting dressed as we speak. What's up with you?" Tasha asked, as she fastens her bra.

"Shit, I'm waiting for the day to go by so we can get to this concert. Bitch, I can't wait. What time you coming over?" Nicole asked, with excitement in her voice.

"Well, I was thinking about four or five o'clock. I'ma clean up, make me something to eat, then I'll be on my way over there," Tasha stated.

Nicole sucked her teeth. "Bitch, by four or five o'clock? I was just over there last night, Tee, and unless you had a party after I dropped you off from the mall, yo house don't need that much cleaning." They shared a laugh. "Plus, I cooked breakfast, so you can just come on over here and eat. I made your favorite." Before Tasha could object, Nicole made the decision for her. "As a matter of fact, I'm on my way to you. I'ma bring you a plate and we can clean up yo place together then come back to my house in my car. That way after the concert I can just drop you off or you can spend the night until later on that morning because we both might be too tired after the concert."

"Damn, bitch! You one on one, huh?" Tasha asked, laughing. "Alright, come on since you got this shit all figured out, but even if I said no, I don't think it would matter, but fuck all that I'm hungry, so hurry yo ass up."

Nicole laughed. "Bitch your plate was being made while we was talking and you're right," Nicole said with a giggle. "It wouldn't have mattered if you'd said no. I'm on my way out the door as we speak, bye. See you in ten minutes, love you."

Tasha giggled. "Bitch, I love you, too."

Tasha ended the call and went to her closet to pick out something to wear. As she got dressed and picked her clothes out for the next two days, she hoped that she would be able to control herself being so close to Billie. Tasha laid the clothes on the bed, and then went to the kitchen and made herself two shots of Parton.

Tasha had just finished her second shot of Parton when her front door flew open. Nicole was smiling from ear to ear with a plate of food in her hand.

"Bitch, where you at? What it do, ho? What the fuck it do?" Nicole yelled as she walked in, kicking the door closed behind her.

Tasha laughed as she came out the kitchen. "What you do, one hundred miles per hour all the way here?"

"Naw, more like one-twenty. A bitch felt like a NASCAR driver when I was weaving in and out of traffic. I'm super on one. I can't wait 'til tomorrow. We gonna be the flyest bitches at that muthafucka."

They both laughed.

Nicole handed Tasha her plate, and went to the hall closet and grabbed the vacuum. "Go 'head and eat, I'll get started with the cleaning."

Tasha took the cover off the plate; her stomach growled as her eyes ran over the layout Nicole had cooked—country fried potatoes, scrambled eggs made with three different cheeses, onions, tomatoes and bell peppers, three turkey sausage links, three pieces of turkey beacon, two homemade biscuits with a side of grits with butter, salt and pepper. Tasha sat at the table, using the plastic spoon and fork Nicole had put with her food. She began eating.

"Bitch, you lucky I ain't a nigga," Tasha stated, stuffing her mouth with potatoes and eggs.

Nicole cut the vacuum off. "Why?" She turned all her attention to her best friend, waiting for a reply.

"Because, bitch, I do like Beyoncé said, and put a ring on it, if you feed me like this every day!"

Nicole started laughing. "Bitch, shut yo ass up!"

Tasha almost choked, laughing at her own joke.

"Yeah bitch, don't die over there trying to clown," Nicole said, making it over to Tasha to pat her on the back.

"Ooh, I'm not, I gotta live for this concert," Tasha said, as she began digging back into her food.

Nicole giggled as she walked into the kitchen putting a plate in the sink she had removed off the counter. Nicole saw the Patron and shot glass; poured herself a shot, she necked it, and ran water in the sink.

"Mmm, I needed that," Nicole stated, feeling her chest burn as she washed the plate off.

Tasha looked over her shoulder. "Bitch don't feel bad, I had two shots before you got here and I needed both of them," Tasha said, while chewing on a piece of sausage. "Damn, yo ass cooks just like your momma."

Nicole laughed. "Thanks girl, but I'm not that good yet."

Tasha finished her plate and took it into the kitchen. Nicole washed it off then took down another shot of Patron as she wiped off the counter.

"Alright, so what's left to do?" Nicole asked as she hung the towel on the towel rack.

"Shit, that's pretty much it," Tasha stated, looking around. "Let me go finish packing my bag and we can be on our way."

Nicole walked into the living room and turned on the CD player. Trey Songz's, "Jupiter Love," came on. She sat down, kicked up her feet and started listening to Trey Songz's "Jupiter Love."

"Go ahead; I'll be right here chilling, waiting on you." Nicole said, feeling the Patron kicking in.

Tasha laughed as she went into her bedroom. "That bitch knows she can't handle no liquor." Tasha grabbed her overnight bag and began putting her pajamas, under garments and the new outfits she had picked out to take with her inside the bag. She grabbed her overnight bag and the outfit she was wearing to the concert and headed back to the living room so she and Nicole could get ready to head to her house.

* * *

Billie had decided to go into the office after eating breakfast. He figured since the concert was on Sunday, Monday he was for sure going to sleep in late. So knowing this, he knew it would be best to tighten up all loose ends, make sure payroll was correct and get the crew's agenda ready so he wouldn't be disturbed by a call Monday morning. He pulled up to his office on La Brea and Fairview at 11:30 AM.

Monica was bent over, filing papers as he walked in. She had on a short dress, and from where Billie stood, he had a clear view of her perfectly shaped ass and full hips; the imprint of her fat pussy could also be seen.

Billie closed the door, which made Monica look over her shoulder. Still bent over with her hand in the file cabinet, she knew she had locked the door and only one other person had keys beside her.

"Hey, boss." She smiled from ear to ear, showing a set of perfect white teeth. "What you doing here on a Saturday?" she asked, glad that he had decided to stop by. Her pussy began throbbing in hopes that she could get some dick to start off her weekend.

Billie walked past Monica, smacking her on her soft but firm ass, which made her pussy wetter.

"Shit, just thought I'd come in today to tighten things up and see what the crew's agenda looks like for Monday, because I'm not coming in."

He sat at his desk and turned on the computer.

Monica stood up and stopped filing the forms she was placing in monthly order and walked over to the coffee pot, making Billie a cup of Green Tea with lemon and honey.

Billie watched her hips and ass sway as his computer warmed up.

Monica had worked for him for the past two years. She found the ad in the paper right after she had gotten her AA in Business from Cal State Northridge. When she first called about the job, Billie had told her he was looking for someone to work full-time and would pay $17.00 an hour, which he will raise to $20.00 after the first three months.

Monica took the address down and the next morning she was the second person there to apply. After thirty minutes, she decided she wanted to be last and went to the end of the line. After five women and two men, Monica stepped in dressed to kill. She had worn a three-piece tan Prada skirt suit with a white butterfly collar DKNY button up shirt. She left the top three buttons unfasten so just a little skin could be shown—*classy, not trashy*, her mother once told her. She wore tan Prada six-inch heels, which made her taller.

CHAPTER 13

NICOLE PHONED BILLIE, AS SHE GOT off the 405 onto La Tijera. It was still early in the day and both she and Tasha needed their hair and nails done. They decided to go to Billie and Zane's homeboy's place—Chuck's Barber Shop & Beauty Salon. It was right by her house, and the nail shop both she and Tasha loved was in the same shopping center. As soon as Billie answered the phone, Nicole started explaining her plans.

"Hey, Daddy, we were going to Chuck's and the nail shop, getting ready for tomorrow," Nicole said, as she pulled into the parking lot.

"What time you think you'll be home?" she asked, as she parked in front of 7-11.

Billie pulled up his pants. "Shit, I gotta get cut up myself, so when I leave the office, I'ma come up to Chuck's. After that, I'll be at the house."

"Okay, Daddy, that's cool, because Tee spending the night, so I want us to kick it like old times."

"Tee's spending the night?" Billie stated aloud, stunned by what he heard. He didn't know he was on the car Bluetooth system.

"Yeah, nigga, I'm spending the night. What, you got a problem with that?" Tasha stated smartly, and rolled her eyes at the phone, as she and Nicole shared a laugh, as the phone went dead silent on Billie's end.

"Hello, Daddy?" Nicole said, after thirty seconds.

"Oh, I'm here," Billie answered, still in a daze.

"What's wrong, you okay?" Nicole asked, feeling concerned.

"Nothing, I just wasn't ready for you to be bringing home any wild animals. Is that bitch house broken?"

Nicole started laughing, as Tasha sucked her teeth, trying to hold back her laughter.

"That shit ain't even that funny, Cola," Tasha said, smiling.

"Yes it is, bitch," Nicole stated, still laughing.

Tasha cleared her throat. "Yeah, okay Mr. Billie's Plumbing Service, but question, are you sure you fix pipes, because the way you be white around the mouth a bitch be wondering do you smoke 'em, with your black stank'n ass," Tasha said, as Nicole started laughing uncontrollable.

"Y'all so damn stupid. Ooh God my stomach hurts, but, umm, yeah, Daddy, she staying over. It'll be better because we wanna get there early."

"I'm cool with that," Billie lied. "Well I'll see y'all in a minute. Love you, Cola."

"I love you too, Daddy."

"Bye, stank ass bitch," Billie said to Tasha.

"Bye, you black ass, nasty, stank ass nigga; you monkey face bastard."

Billie laughed. "Ooh you mad, Tee?"

"Naw, nigga, I'ma get you back tonight, you know what it is. Real bitches get even!"

"I feel you, so with that being said; I can take it that I won round one. So fuck you. Get even with that," Billie said, hanging up with laughter.

"Ooooooow, he makes me so sick," Tasha said, as she and Nicole got out the car laughing.

"Yeah, I know he does," Nicole said, as they walked into Chuck's, telling Lisa—the hairdresser—they needed her to hook them up.

"But that's why y'all get along so well, because both of y'all crazy and got jokes."

Lisa told them she could get to them in an hour, which was perfect. They told her they would be next door getting their nails and feet done and would be back in an hour.

*   *   *   *   *

Billie sat at his desk in deep thought. He wasn't expecting to be so close to Tasha so soon. He didn't know how he would react to her now that they had sex and he didn't want Nicole to see the difference in the way they were toward each other.

Damn, I hope Tee can make this shit work, he thought, as Monica came out the bathroom and headed back toward him.

"So you done on the phone?" She smiled.

"Yeah, but I'ma have to go and get my hair cut for tomorrow."

Monica frowned. "So I guess, I'll see you Tuesday, huh?" she asked, disappointment written all over her face.

Billie stood up and kissed her on the lips. "Yeah Tuesday, but remember, me and you in Cancun."

Monica smiled. "Promise?" she asked, bouncing up and down on her tippy toes, which made Billie laugh.

"I promise. Now I need to know that you got my back. You gonna hold this shit down for a nigga, right?"

Monica grabbed his shirt, pulled him to her and stuck her tongue in his mouth, and ended the kiss by softly sucking his bottom lip.

"Don't I always?" she asked, seductively, releasing his shirt.

"Yeah, you do," Billie replied, smiling at her. "That's why I love you so much!"

Monica's heart skipped a beat.

Billie grabbed his keys and headed for the door. Monica's mind was racing, she had wanted to tell him how she truly felt about him and here he was saying it to her. It didn't matter to Monica if he meant it or not, or if he was joking. All that mattered was he said it. The bar door slamming snapped her out her trance. She took off walking as fast as she could to catch him. She made it to the door just as he was pulling off.

"Fuck!" Monica yelled out through the door, hitting it with her fists. "I love you, too," she yelled, as he pulled out on to Fairview. "I fuckin' love you, too!"

Billie pulled into the parking lot of Chuck's just as a black Range Rover was pulling out, freeing a parking place directly in front of the nail shop. As Billie pulled in the parking space, he saw Tasha sitting in the spa chair inside the nail shop. Tasha saw him as well. She pulled her dress up slightly, and opened her legs so Billie could see her panties. Billie sat there shaking his head.

He started looking through the window of the nail shop trying to locate Nicole. He spotted her on the far right getting her feet done and in a deep conversation with the woman doing them.

Billie looked back at Tasha, who was waiting for him to give her his attention again. She looked around real quick and when she was sure no one was paying her any mind, she reached underneath her dress, pulled her thong to the side and rubbed her clit, and licked her finger and smiled at Billie. Billie's dick got hard, as they maintained eye contact, but lost in their own thoughts. Their eye contact was finally broken when one of the nail shop workers came over and sat down in front of Tasha to do her feet. Tasha closed her legs and winked at Billie, as he got out the car.

"What the fuck have I gotten myself into?" Billie asked himself, as he fixed his dick so it wouldn't be noticeable to the world. He closed the car door and walked into the nail shop. Nicole, seeing her man, began smiling.

"Hey, Daddy," she said, ready to jump out her chair for a hug.

The woman doing her feet grabbed her legs, so she wouldn't get up. "Me no finish. One minute!" the Korean lady stated, and returned to French tipping Nicole's toes.

Nicole calmed down, as Billie walked over to her, giving her a kiss on the lips.

"What's up, beautiful?" he asked, as he broke the kiss.

"You, that's what up," Nicole replied, still smiling.

"Well, I'ma go next door to Chuck's and get my hair cut while you two over here. I love you!"

"I love you, too, Daddy."

Billie gave Nicole another kiss and headed toward the door to leave.

"Hey, Tee, catch," Billie said, causing Tasha's eyes to dart toward him, as she held out her hands in front of her, as she noticed him giving her the bird.

"Ooh like that?" Tasha asked, giggling, as she put her hand back on her lap feeling foolish for not paying more attention.

"Yeah, like that and once again, I win!"

Nicole started laughing, as Billie walked out the door with his hands over his head, pumping his fist up and down.

"I swear," Tasha said, laughing. "I'ma get his ass back," she told Nicole who was still laughing, but now holding her stomach. "Oooow, he makes me so damn sick," Tasha said, rolling her eyes and laughing again, as the nail lady finished her feet.

As Chuck was finishing Billie's haircut, Nicole and Tasha walked into the shop. Every man that was waiting for their turn to get a haircut turned to admire their beauty, even a few of the women looked their way, hating. Chuck gave Billie dap.

"Yo bitch is bad, my nigga, and so is her girl," Chuck stated, now dusting Billie off.

Billie laughed, as he watched all the men in the shop lusting over his woman and his now side bitch, Tasha. He saw Chuck's wife, Lisa, going to greet them.

"True, but Lisa is fine as hell, too," Billie replied, watching Lisa's ass giggle and her hips sway, as she walked over to Nicole and Tasha, hugged them both and took them over to the sinks so she could start washing their hair.

"Yeah, I know, but shit always looks better when it's someone else's," Chuck said, handing Billie a mirror so he could check out his cut.

"Plus, look how niggas still eyeing them," Chuck stated, still looking himself.

"The only reason they still doing that is because these niggas don't know Cola's my girl and Tasha's my friend. Trust me; if these niggas didn't know Lisa was your wife, they'd be eyeballing her, too. Lisa is eye candy fo' sho," Billie said, handing Chuck back the mirror. He reached in his pocket, pulling out thirty dollars and giving him eighteen for the cut and twelve for the tip.

"I must agree with you there, my nigga," Chuck said, as he stuck the money in his pocket. Chuck removed the smock from around Billie's neck. They embraced, and gave each other a pound.

"Get at me, dogg," Chuck said, as a plan began to form in Billie's mind.

"Fo' sho that's man down," Billie replied, looking at Chuck with a devilish grin.

"Ay, my nigga, watch this move I'm 'bout to put down."

Chuck shook his head, knowing Billie was up to no good, as he watched him walk over to the shampoo bowls where Nicole and Tasha were waiting to get their hair washed. Men in the shop were still watching Nicole and Tasha, as they held a conversation, waiting for Lisa to get them.

Confidence written all over his face, Billie approached Tasha first who, to everybody who didn't know them, looked like he was getting dissed. Whatever he said to Tasha caused her to kick him in the knee before telling him to get away from her. All the niggas looking on laughed.

"Shorty ain't no joke," one man stated while still laughing.

Chuck, Lisa and his workers laughed. They knew this was the norm with Tasha and Billie. Billie shot Tasha the bird.

"You ain't all that anyway," he said aloud, causing niggas in the shop to make sounds and smart remarks.

"Shit, yes she is," one short light-skinned nigga stated.

The younger guy next to him said, "He just mad, cuz. Shorty dissed his ass!"

This was just what Billie wanted to happen. He smiled, as he walked over to Nicole, rubbing his knee. Nicole was laughing, but she stopped when Billie began talking to her. Everybody in the shop was silent, trying to hear what he was saying to her, but the only sound were clippers humming, as someone got their haircut. Nicole giggled at something Billie told her. He leaned in and whispered in her ear. As he was pulling away from her ear, she grabbed his shirt and gave him a kiss.

"I'm holding you to that," she said aloud before releasing him.

"Babe, like my nigga, T.I., said, you can have whatever you like," Billie stated, and stole another kiss before he walked toward the doors, making his exit.

Niggas in the shop gave Billie high-fives, as he walked out the door. Billie looked at Chuck who was smiling.

"You a fool, my nigga," Chuck said, throwing up the deuces, as Billie walked out the door.

"I know," Billie said with a wink and throwing up the deuces. He took a quick glance at Tasha who was mean mugging him. He made a kissing sound with his lips and gave her a wink, as he pointed to his ass.

Tasha rolled her eyes and sucked her teeth, as Billie disappeared. *Ooow, he gets on my damn nerves*, she thought as she and Nicole started laughing.

Tasha and Nicole were still laughing when Lisa walked over to them.

"Billie's ass still crazy," Lisa said, as she put Tasha's head in the sink and began rinsing it.

"Yeah, he ain't changed since grade school," Nicole said, giggling, thinking back to the old days.

Tasha, feeling the warm water hit her hair, exhaled.

"And he still makes me sick," Tasha stated, and started laughing.

"Y'all always been at each other for as long as I can remember," Lisa said, as she recalled their days in Junior high school.

Lisa, Chuck, Tasha, Billie and Nicole went to school together.

"And from what I'm remembering, y'all three have always been like The Three Musketeers."

They shared another laugh, as Lisa turned her attention from Tasha to Nicole.

With her head still in the sink, Tasha closed her eyes, as Nicole was getting her hair washed. She became lost in thought thinking about Billie, her pussy got wet when she seen Billie walking over to her, if she hadn't kicked him when she did, she probably would of reach for him and kissed him herself.

Ooh my God, this nigga got me all fucked up in the head, Tasha thought, as she remembered him making love to her in her bed. Her pussy throbbed, as she recalled him holding her as they slept. She was brought back to reality when Lisa wrapped a towel around her head.

"Come on, Tee," Lisa said, as she helped Tasha out her seat and led her toward her booth. "Let's get this long beautiful hair of yours hooked up."

Tasha smiled at Lisa, but said a silent prayer, as she sat in the chair to get her hair pressed.

Lord, please give me the strength," Tasha thought, as she felt the wetness of her pussy moistening her thighs. *In the name of Jesus, give me the strength, Father, while I'm at their house to control my hunger for this man.* Tasha closed her eyes, as Lisa began running the pressing comb through her hair.

CHAPTER 14

AS BILLIE PULLED IN HIS DRIVEWAY, he realized he still hadn't told Nicole about the new plumbing deal. He took a deep breath, exhaled and relaxed in his seat feeling more confused than he had ever felt in his whole twenty-nine years on earth. He turned the volume up to enjoy his Kendrick Lamer CD, as he thought about how he really had feelings for Tasha. Billie was starting to realize he even loved her and was concluding that over the years all the joking and playing was his way for showing his true feelings without really saying it. He thought back to junior high and senior high school. He remembered how he felt about Tasha then. She was the coolest girl he knew and was with the business. When Nicole finally gave him a chance that he never really was expecting, he repressed the feelings he had for Tasha. He had to. Now fifteen years later, here they were, slapping him in his face.

"What's a nigga to do?" Billie asked himself, as he hopped out the car and headed for the front door.

He loved Nicole. Nicole was like Tasha in so many ways, but she was also different in even more. Billie could talk to Nicole, but with Tasha, he could express himself freely. They had developed a close bond without even realizing it. Billie always had opened up to Tasha. Tasha never judged him, nor tried to clown what he felt. Tasha would always give thought to his questions and give him answers that he would have thought of. They thought alike and Tasha was more open whereas Nicole was more repressed. Billie remembered how they would sit in all their classes and talk about any and everything.

I loved her then, Billie thought, as he walked into his front door, closed the door and went into the kitchen and grabbed the Patron. He took the top off and began drinking from the bottle, as he headed to his game room.

"A nigga is going to have to control himself, his thoughts and his feelings tonight while Tasha is here," he said aloud, taking another drink from the bottle, as he entered his game room.

Deciding on changing clothes he made a U-turn, walked into his bedroom, took another stiff drink from the bottle. Billie sat the bottle on the bed, as he took off his clothes and went into the bathroom taking a quick shower. Once done he dried off, smoothed on lotion, put on some deodorant, threw on some sweats and a tee shirt and picked up his Patron bottle off the bed taking another long swig, as he headed back to his game room.

Once inside, he dropped into his game chair, cut on his PS3 and began playing Black Ops. He needed to free his mind and relax. He put his headset on, took a long drink from his newfound friend and comforter, grabbed his remote and, feeling faded, he entered his user name.

*   *   *   *   *

Nicole and Tasha stepped out of Chuck's Barber Shop and Beauty Salon feeling like a million bucks. All eyes were on them, as they walked to Nicole's Jag and got in.

"Bitch, we look good girl. That Ho Lisa knows she can do some hair," Nicole said, as she started the car and looked at herself in her rear view mirror.

Tasha pulled down the sun visor, looking herself over in the mirror.

"We do look good," she agreed. "We some supa fly ass bitches!"

They gave each other a high-five, as Nicole pulled out the parking lot. Tasha pushed the visor back up, as Nicole cut the air conditioner on. A light-skinned brotha in an F-150 damn near ran the red light looking in their car smiling at them. They laughed.

"That nigga is thirsty," Tasha stated laughing, as Nicole turned on Alvern.

"They can't help but want a drink of our big gulps," Nicole said, in a matter of fact tone. "We some bad ass bitches! Now let's go old school on his scrub. If you fine and you know it, clap yo hands." They both clapped their hands, as Nicole pulled in the driveway and started laughing, as she cut the car off.

They both stepped out the car and Tasha picked up where Nicole left off.

"If you fine and you know it, then your attitude will surely show it, if you fine and you know it, make that ass clap."

They both bent over, put their hands on their knees bent over and made their asses clap laughing.

"Bitch yo ass is crazy, you got a bitch on her block making her ass clap."

"So what, bitch, we can do that," Tasha said, smiling, as they walked to the front door. As Nicole was opening the door, Tasha noticed Mr. Green the older man who lived across the street watching them. Tasha, with a devilish smirk on her face, bent over and lifted her dress, letting him see her beautiful perfectly shaped ass, and she slapped herself on her left cheek and winked at him.

Nicole heard the sound of someone or something being slapped, and turned around just in time to see what Tasha was doing.

"Bitch, yo ass is so wrong," Nicole stated, laughing, as Tasha pulled her dress down and blew a kiss to Mr. Green, who had dropped the water hose and was standing there looking with his mouth wide open. They stepped in the house both laughing at Mr. Green's reaction.

"Bitch, you going to give that old man a heart attack," Nicole stated, as they both sat on the sofa.

"Shit, he was staring so I decided to give him something to stare at," Tasha said, giggling. "Plus, that probably made his year."

Nicole started laughing.

"Girl, he is so damn nasty. Bitch, every time he sees me he be like 'Hah little mommy, I know your man can't handle all of you. If I was forty years younger, I'd take you from him girl.' I just smile and brush him off. But a few days ago when I got up and went outside to get the morning paper…well, Mr. Green was sweeping his driveway, and I had on my white robe with my panties and bra underneath. I bent over feeling myself and gave his old horny ass a view of my backside. I picked the paper up then turned around to face him and said Hi in my sexiest voice. Bitch, he had stopped sweeping. His little dick was standing straight out through his pants. I put my paper under my arms, licked my lips and told him if I was twenty years older, I'd have my way with him, then I walked to my door swaying my hips and ass so that every step I took my ass jiggled. Bitch, when I closed the door, I looked through the blinds to see what his reaction was. His old ass had his hand in his pants playing with his dick."

They both started laughing.

"Now bitch, that was wrong," Tasha stated, holding her stomach, still laughing. "He probably be telling all his old buddies how he be getting play from two young fine bitches."

They started laughing again.

"Well bitch, the guest bedroom is down that hall so you can go put your stuff up. I'ma go put my, I'm at home clothes on. I'll be right back to help you unpack."

As Nicole went upstairs, Tasha walked out the front door to retrieve her things from the car. What she saw made her laugh aloud. Mr. Green had his hand in his pants, she could see his hand moving back and forward through his jeans. When he noticed her, he took off into his house leaving the water hose running on the lawn. Tasha continued to laugh grabbing her bags out the trunk.

"Nasty old bastard," she said, as she walked back into the house giggling with her bags in her hand.

CHAPTER 15

NICOLE MADE IT BACK DOWNSTAIRS WEARING her Super Woman boy shorts and wife-beater to match just as Tasha was hanging her clothes in the guest room closet.

"Hey girl," Nicole said, walking into the room smiling, "What to do!"

Tasha laughed, "Bitch I'm putting my shit up, that's what it do," she replied, hanging the last item of clothing that needed to be put in the closet.

Nicole sat on the bed and Tasha took off her clothes, reached in her carryon bag and pulled out her Bat Girl wife-beater and boy shorts. Then while placing them on...

"Bitch, I got that movie, The Call, with Halle Berry on DVD," Tasha said, as she sat next to Nicole, looking through her bag for the movie.

"For real, girl? How you come up on that?" Nicole asked, looking over her shoulder.

"You know Tina's nigga go to all the previews. Anyway, she sold me one for ten dollars."

Tasha found the movie and looked at Nicole smiling.

"Let's go watch this shit, I heard it's off the chain," they jumped off the bed and went into the living room.

Tasha placed the movie in the DVD player, as Nicole went into the kitchen to put the popcorn in the microwave, grabbed the Red Vines and get the drinks. Tasha came into the kitchen helping Nicole bring the Red Vines and the drinks into the living room while Nicole waited for the popcorn to finish popping.

"Is Billie going to watch the movie with us?" Tasha asked, sitting the Red Vines on the floor and placing the drinks on the end table.

"Let's go find out," Nicole replied, as she walked in with the popcorn, sitting it on the sofa and headed upstairs with Tasha right behind her heading to Billie's game room.

Billie was playing his PS3 giving orders over his headset when Nicole and Tasha came in and stood in front of the TV placing their hands on their hips.

"Excuse us, but we want to know if you are coming downstairs to watch *The Call* with us," Nicole said, cocking her head to the side.

Billie paused the game; he was stunned momentarily at the beauty of the two women blocking his TV. Tasha's smart comment brought him back to reality.

"I no damn well yo stank ass heard what Cola asked you," Tasha said, grabbing a pillow whacking him up side his head, knocking Billie's headset off his head.

"Oh you got the game fucked up, Tee," Billie stated, as he jumped up grabbing her and throwing her on the sofa.

Tasha laughed, as she was slammed on the sofa, she jumped back up just as Nicole grabbed the other pillow and caught Billie on the other side of his head making him trip over the arm of the sofa. He fell on the floor and both Nicole and Tasha was on him raining blow after blow with the pillows not giving him a chance to get up. Billie had no choice but to cover his face and ball up.

"Oh, so y'all getting down like that?" he asked laughing, still trying to block their blows.

"Yeah nigga, who winning now," Tasha asked, placing her foot on his back, as she tried to hit him in the face? Nicole was standing in front of him raining blow after blow to the top of his head.

"Alright, alright," Billie said, seeing he was at a disadvantage. "Y'all win."

"Say it louder," Tasha ordered, now putting pressure on his back with her foot.

"Aaah, okay, okay, y'all win," he yelled, laughing.

Nicole stopped hitting him and put her foot by his face.

"Kiss the queen's feet," she ordered, holding the pillow in her right hand ready to smack him with it if he didn't obey.

"Ahh, hell naw, I'm—"

Tasha whacked him with the pillow, cutting his sentence short.

"Nigga, do as you told," she ordered, and just for good measures, whacked him again.

Billie looked up at Tasha and over to Nicole.

"Yeah alright, but this shit ain't over with—"

Smack!

"Shut the fuck up," Tasha said, after hitting him again. "Now get to kissing."

Billie kissed Nicole's left foot.

"That's right," Nicole said, as she removed it and lifted her right foot so it could be kissed, as well.

"Oh you bitches doing—"

Smack, smack!

Nicole and Tasha both hit him with their pillows. Get to kissing they said together, smiling at him. Billie gave them a devilish smile, and kissed Nicole's right foot.

"Now, roll over on your stomach," Tasha ordered, and helped him obey by kicking him with her foot.

"Yeah, y'all got this round," Billie stated, now on his stomach.

Nicole and Tasha looked at each other laughing.

"Have your ass down stairs in five minutes, nigga," Nicole ordered, laughing.

"Yeah, alright you got that," Billie replied, already plotting his revenge.

Tasha looked at Nicole and giggled. She smacked Billie with her pillow and took off running. Nicole followed suit doing the same, as they ran down the stairs they both said in unison.

"We won, nigga!" As they descended the stairs, still laughing, they heard Billie yell.

"Y'all know this means war!"

Both Nicole and Tasha turned around to see Billie standing at the top of the stairs mad, dogging them with an evil smile on his face. Tasha smiled; it matched the one on Billie's face. She put her hands on her hips and cocked her head to the side.

"Nigga, fuck yo threats. Bring it!"

Nicole gave Tasha a high-five and they walked into the kitchen to make another bowl of popcorn, leaving Billie there laughing.

"It's on now," he said to himself aloud. "It's muthafuckin' on!"

Billie walked into his and Nicole's bedroom. He went into his closet and pulled out his Super Soaker water gun. He laughed to himself.

"Y'all bitches done fucked up," he said, as he went into the bathroom to fill up the forty-gallon backpack that came with the gun. Once filled, he looked down the stairs to see if Nicole and Tasha were in sight. He snuck down the stairs taking them one by one. About half way down he heard them laughing in the kitchen.

"Yeah, laugh now, but I promise y'all bitches going to be mad later," he said, laughing as he descended the stairs, ran over to the sofa in the living room, hid his Super Soaker behind the sofa, and sat on the sofa grabbing a Red Vine and eating it.

Nicole and Tasha walked in with the second bowl of popcorn just as Billie was finishing the Red Vine.

"I'm glad you decided to follow the queen's orders," Nicole said, with a smile.

"Yeah, we glad you listened, because we would of loved if you didn't, because that would of made us have to come get your AZZ!"

Billie smiled, "Yeah, y'all got that round, I submit."

Tasha sucked her teeth. "What the fuck ever, nigga. It ain't ever that easy, but we ready for your little revenge. Ain't nobody stupid!"

"Naw, y'all got that. I'm just here to enjoy the movie with my two favorite girls," Billie said, smiling.

Nicole looked at Tasha, and they both looked at Billie.

"Nigga, please," they said together, and started laughing.

Tasha grabbed the remote and pressed play, as Nicole handed Billie a bowl of popcorn and sat next to Tasha on the floor right, as the movie was about to start, Billie put a handful of popcorn in his mouth.

"Ooh, I just want you both to know," he said while chewing making both of them look back, "Y'all hair look really nice."

They smiled.

"Thank you, Daddy," Nicole said, turning back around.

Tasha gave Billie the bird. "Nigga, I know!"

Nicole laughed, as Tasha turned back around.

As Billie looked over the side of the sofa, a devilish smile crossed his face, as he saw his Super Soaker in its hiding place. *I got something for yo smart mouth,* he thought as he turned back and faced the TV. *Revenge is so sweet.* He threw another handful of popcorn in his mouth, as Halle Berry answered her first 911 call.

CHAPTER 16

THE MOVIE WAS NONSTOP ACTION FROM the beginning to the end.

"That movie was the business," Billie said, chewing on a Red Vine.

"I know. Did you see how Halle Berry went looking for the victim? She's a real ride or die bitch for that," Nicole stated, smiling.

"Yeah, in a way, but it's her fault the white bitch got caught, plus Halle was scared. How you going to go after a killer with no weapon, then get to his house and freeze up? Who does that? She did okay, but she should of went there ready for whatever, see if they had a bitch like me playing that part, I would of went after his ass packing and ready for war," Tasha stated, using her fingers as a gun.

"So what else do we got to watch?" Billie asked, reaching his arm behind the sofa.

Tasha stood up, I brought, G.I. Joe, The Revenge of Cobra, you know the one with The Rock in it," Tasha said, headed to the guess bedroom. "I'ma grab it."

"Oh that's the B.I.," Billie said, grabbing another Red Vine with his free hand. "I heard its better than the first one with Marlin Wayans in it."

Nicole turned toward him and smiled, "You want some more popcorn, Daddy?"

Billie couldn't have asked for better timing, "Please if you don't mind, Pooh."

Nicole jumped up grabbing the empty bowl, and headed to the kitchen. Of course I don't mind, I'll be right back."

Billie watched her ass and hips for a second, retrieved the Super Soaker from behind the sofa and placed the forty-gallon pack on his back.

"I'ma go take a piss, I'll be right back," he yelled, as he snuck down the hallway sneaking up on Tasha.

"Okay Daddy," Nicole yelled from the kitchen, as he got to the door of the guest bedroom. It was wide open; Tasha was bent over looking in her bag for the movie. Billie's dick got hard seeing her ass and pussy in the air. He got a grip on himself, and cleared his throat which made Tasha look over her shoulder, her eyes got big as a dear caught in headlights when she realized what was about to happen.

"Yeah bitch, I told you I'd get you back," Billie said, smiling.

"Ooh no Billie my—"

Splash.

He hit her with a gallon of water.

"Nigga, no you…"

Splash.

He hit her with another gallon.

"Ooh my god, this ain't— "

Splash.

Billie was laughing, as he sprayed her again. Just as he was about to hit her with another gallon of water, he heard Nicole coming up the hall.

"What's so fun— Ooh hell naw," Nicole said, seeing the water gun in Billie's hand. She dropped the bowl and took off running for safety. Billie hit Tasha with another gallon of water and went after Nicole. Nicole had made it to the kitchen and was trying to get out the glass doors when Billie caught up to her.

"Yeah, now what," Billie said, closing the gap between them smiling.

Nicole still fumbling with the door turned around when seeing she couldn't open it and put her hands in the air.

"Daddy, please, I'm sorry my hair, please!"

"Naw fuck all that," he said, hitting her with a gallon of water.

"Ooh my god, no you—"

Splash.

He hit her with another gallon.

Nicole started laughing, "You fucking up my goddamn hair nig—"

Splash.

"Okay, okay," Nicole said, as she spat out a mouth full of water.

"Okay what," Billie asked, looking at her smiling.

"Y'all can't fuck with me. Say it!"

Just as he was about to hit her with another gallon of water, Tasha came up from behind him with the bathroom trashcan filled with water.

"Nigga, fuck you," she said, as she threw the water on him.

"All fuck," Billie yelled, as he tried to dodge the water. He slipped on the water that was on the floor from him wetting Nicole and caught the whole trashcan of water in his face.

"Get up Cola," Tasha said, as she ran to the sink, grabbed the water sprayer that was connected to it.

Nicole tried to get up, but Billie sprayed her with a gallon of water.

"Okay, okay," Nicole said, laughing, "Damn you."

Tasha was now shooting water at him with the sink sprayer while he was still on the floor.

Billie turned toward Tasha, pointing his gun at her. The water Tasha was shooting at him was hitting him in his face and chest, but was no match for his super soaker. He sprayed a gallon at her making her drop the sink sprayer.

"Alright," Tasha yelled, as he hit her with a second gallon.

"Alright, shit stop playing," she screamed.

Nicole seeing he wasn't paying her any attention took action and yanked his water hoses a loose that was connected to the pack and the gun. Billie felt the tug and looked back to see his gun was disconnected and Nicole holding the hoses in her hand. He laughed, as he saw Tasha get back to her feet.

"Oh, now it's on," she said, walking over to him.

With Nicole now on her feet, they were closing in on him.

"Ay, umm, look y'all started it," he said, with a smirk on his face.

"Naw nigga, you done fucked up our hair," Tasha stated, now standing over him.

"Yeah, you done made it to where a bitch gotta do double work," Nicole said, now standing over him as well.

They both were soaking wet, their nipples were hard and showing through their wife-beater t-shirts. They were looking sexy as fuck. Billie's dick got rock hard as he backed up against the glass doors.

"Yo black ass knows the concert is tomorrow, you did this shit on purpose," Tasha said, eyeing him.

Billie laughed, "You damn right, I did. Fuck Trey Songz and y'all hair."

Oh you're jealous because we were looking cute for Trey Songz," Nicole asked, smiling. The thought of him being jealous made her pussy wet.

"Not no more," Billie replied, laughing louder.

"See, Cola, that's why we gonna do him in, right? Now he's evil. Watch his ass real quick." Tasha picked up the trashcan and went to the sink.

"Nigga, you fucked up," she said, as she was filling the trashcan with water and dish washing liquid.

Billie grabbed his dick making Nicole lick her lips.

"Daddy's sorry," Billie whispered slowly getting up off the floor.

"Are you really?" Nicole asked, feeling her pussy tingle.

Tasha looked over her shoulder. "Yeah, I'ma... don't let his scandalous ass get up, Cola, it's a trick," Tasha yelled from the sink.

Nicole looked over her shoulder at Tasha.

"No Tee, he said he—"

Nicole turned around, as she heard the sliding doors open.

"Fuck," she yelled trying to grab Billie through them.

"Fuck both of y'all." Billie laughed as he dove in the pool. "Fuck you bitches!"

"See, I told you Cola," Tasha said, turning off the water faucet.

"Fuck y'all," Billie yelled, laughing; now floating on his back in the pool.

Nicole looked at Tasha and they both started laughing.

"We could lock him out," Nicole said, still laughing.

"Naw, that wouldn't do shit to him. His ass ran out there so he ain't trippin on being out side," Tasha stated, looking at Billie mocking them by waving his middle finger their way, as he floated on his back.

"That's true girl, you're right, so what should we do," Nicole asked, looking at her best friend.

Tasha looked out at Billie and back at Nicole.

"Let's go get our man—"

Tasha and Nicole took off out the door together going to get Billie for fucking up their hair. Billie was still teasing them when he noticed them running toward him.

"Ay, what the fuck are y'all up to?" he yelled at them, as Nicole dove into the pool.

Billie caught off guard by their actions tried to swim to the other end of the pool. Nicole and Tasha had planned on him doing just that. Just as he was all most at the other end, he heard a splash. He looked up to see Tasha.

"And just where do you think you're going," Tasha asked, smiling?

"Yeah," Nicole asked, on the other side of him.

"Why you trying to run off? This is about to get interesting."

Billie was now between them; caught in a sandwich. "Alright, y'all got a nigga cornered. What y'all going to do?"

Nicole smiled. "I got an idea, she said, getting all the way up on him. She kissed him, and put her hand in his pajamas and grabbed his balls.

"Ah that hurt, Cola," he said, frowning.

"I know it did," Nicole replied, still holding his nuts in her hand. "Tee get out the pool real quick for me."

Tasha laughed. "What you doing, bitch? I know that look in your eyes," Tasha said, getting out the pool.

Nicole winked at Tasha.

"Ooh, you're going to love this, nigga. Take yo shirt off," Nicole demanded.

Billie looked Nicole in her eyes. "Take my shirt off for... awww," he moaned in pain, as Nicole applied a little pressure to his nuts. "Okay, Cola," Billie said, pulling his shirt over his head.

"Now throw it to Tee."

He threw it to Tasha. Tasha laughed as she caught it.

"Now pull your pajama pants off," Nicole ordered, stilling holding on to his balls.

"Cola, you trippin'...awww, okay, okay," he pulled his pajama pants off and held them up.

"Now throw them to Tee."

Tasha caught them with a smile on her face.

"Tee, go cut the fog lights on," Nicole said, still looking at Billie.

Tasha ran in the house and cut the fog lights on, the whole back yard lit up.

"Now I'ma let you go okay, but if you move, I'ma scream rape so loud that everybody on the block will hear me. Do you understand?"

Billie laughed.

"You're an evil bitch."

"Yeah I know, I can be when pushed and you just pushed me, but that's neither here nor there. Do you understand what I just said?"

"Yeah I understand," Billie said, with a smirk on his face.

"Alright now be a good boy," Nicole let go of his balls, swam toward Tasha and got out the pool. They both started laughing, as they walked to the glass door and went inside them. When they turned around to lock the doors Billie was looking at them smiling.

"A Cola, you know I don't have a problem being out here naked." Billie said, still smiling.

"Ooh, you will in a few minutes," Nicole stated with a wicked smile on her face, as she closed the blinds and grabbed the phone.

"Cola what the fuck you mean by that," Billie yelled, still able to see their frames through the closed blinds. Billie sat there for a minute lost in thought on what she could mean.

"Who the fuck you on the phone with Cola," Billie yelled, now getting mad because he couldn't figure out what was going on?

Tasha was eyeing her best friend. Nicole opened the blinds and held up a finger, telling him to hold up, and closed them back as the phone was answered.

"Hello 911, what's your emergency?"

"Hi, my name is Nicole White. There is a naked man in my pool!"

"Okay Ms. White, we will send a car out."

"Thank you so much," Nicole said, and hung up the phone and started laughing.

Tasha was standing there with her mouth wide open in shock.

"Nah, ah, Cola, no you didn't. You a cold bitch," Tasha said, and started laughing.

"Yeah I am, but tonight we win."

They high-fived each other laughing, as they walked away from the glass doors just as they heard Billie starting to knock on them declaring that they won and begging them to please let him in.

CHAPTER 17

IT WAS 7:30 PM WHEN MONICA walked into her mother's house. She had left the office and didn't want to go home because she didn't want to be alone. Monica wanted Billie there with her, but as the second wheel better known as, girlfriend number two. She had to stay in her lane until the time was right.

"Damn it, why did he have to say he loved me," Monica stated aloud, as she walked toward the kitchen. She could smell her mother's cooking when she drove up.

"Hey Momma," Monica said, as she entered the kitchen.

"Hey baby," Ms. Williams replied without turning around from her pot of Gumbo.

Monica walked up behind her mom giving her a kiss on the cheek.

"I thought I heard you come in. How is my baby?"

"I'm fine Mom. Mommy, I'm in love," Monica answered, and exhaled, as she fell into a chair at the kitchen table.

"I think I'm in love," her mother laughed. "Child, I been knew that," her mother said in a matter fact tone.

Monica laughed, "Whatever Mommy!"

"Girl you my only child, I know more than you think. It's that fine hunk of chocolate you work for."

Monica grasped, "Momma!"

"Momma, what? Girl I was your age once. Shit ain't nothing to be a shame of, he is a good man. He ain't bad looking either, plus he cares about you and wants what best for you. So go for what you know, because if you don't, believe you me some other little heffa will."

Monica laughed, "Momma, he got a woman that lives with him."

"And," Ms. Williams asked her daughter turning around to face her. "If he was so in love with that bitch he lives with you can trust and believe he wouldn't be spending the night at your house, helping you buy a car, nor helping you live right. He doesn't know what he wants, just like most men don't. You have to show him not only what he wants, but you're what he needs. When you daddy was alive, I made sure he knew he needed me. He never strayed away from home a whole twenty-four hours...

never, because he knew that he could get all his wants filled right here. Now I'm not going to say he didn't cheat, because men will be men, but I didn't know about it, nor did he let it come back to me because he knew what he had at home. At the end of the day, he knew I was going to be here. I was going to do whatever he needed done and I was what he needed, as a matter of fact. I can't say he didn't cheat; he loved us and gave us everything. So that bitch ain't doing something right that's why he's at your door and in your bed. Now if you want him, show him you're what he needs and I promise you, you'll have him."

Monica laughed. "Mommie, I didn't know you had game like that."

"Child please, you must remember I been your age before, you ain't never been mine."

They shared a laugh. Monica smelled the crab legs her mother was now chopping up and her stomach turned. She got up and ran to the bathroom. Monica made it to the toilet just in time, as the sandwich she ate for lunch came up. Monica sat on the floor hugging the toilet, as her mother walked to the door.

"Umm hmm, and you need to go to the doctor, because if I'm not mistaken, and I'm sure I'm not, you about to give me a grandbaby."

Monica looked up at her mother and put her head back in the toilet.

Her mother laughed. "Yeah, he been hitting that pussy without a condom. You're what he wants and needs and that's why he ain't been putting a hat on his little man. Now you're about to have his baby. Go get your man and my new son-in-law." Ms. Williams walked back to the kitchen, leaving her daughter in the bathroom still hugging the toilet.

CHAPTER 18

NICOLE AND TASHA STOOD BY ONE of the police cars giggling, as the police officer went into the back yard to get the naked man out their pool.

"Ooh my God, Cola. You wrong for this shit," Tasha said, now laughing, as the officers came through the back gate with Billie wrapped in a blanket.

Nicole turned her head so the officers wouldn't see her laughing. Nicole turned back around when she got control of herself.

"His black ass shouldn't have fucked our hair up," Tasha stated, covering her mouth, as she giggled. They watched, as the police escorted Billie to one of the cars and placed him inside while he was trying to explain he owned the house.

"Yeah, I bet you do," one of the officers remarked smartly, as he closed the door.

Nicole was playing her part like she was trying to win a Grammy ran over to the police car that they had just, put Billie in.

"Ooh my God, it's my husband," she said, as Billie mad dogged her through the window.

Now confused, the officer looked at Nicole. "So you know him?"

"Oh yes, I know him, officer. Oh God, I should have checked before I called the police," Nicole said, faking distress.

"No, ma'am, you did right by calling us first, because what if it wasn't your husband? You could have been in danger."

Nicole sighed, as the officer let Billie out the car. "I guess you're right," Nicole said, holding back her laughter, as Billie got out the car wrapped in a wool blanket with Los Angeles County Sheriff Department on it in big white letters.

"Sir, I'm sorry about the inconvenience," the officer said to Billie still holding the door open.

Billie looked at Nicole and down the street at Tasha standing by the other car smiling at him.

"Ooh, it's no problem, Sir. You were only doing your job." Billie replied heading toward his front door. He stepped into his front door leaving it wide open. Nicole and Tasha thanked the police and when they drove off, they started laughing, as they went into the house.

"His pride is hurt," Tasha said, as Nicole closed the door.

"Girl I could see the defeat in his eyes," Nicole said and locked the door. They started laughing again.

"Bitch, he is mad," Tasha said, and noticed Billie standing half way up the stairs. She tapped Nicole and pointed up the stairs. Billie had on some sweats with no shirt.

"See that's where y'all wrong at," Billie said, with a devilish smirk on his face that gave both of them goose bumps. "I'm not mad, y'all did that. Oh, but pay back is a bitch!" He laughed, as he went back into his room. "Y'all won that round fo' sho," he yelled, as he grabbed a wife-beater and came down the stairs putting it on. Once at the bottom he stood in front of them.

"So Daddy, we even now," Nicole asked shyly?

Billie laughed. "Yeah if you think we are."

Tasha sucked her teeth. "Well whatever, nigga. We ain't going to kiss your ass. Do what you do!"

Billie laughed. "Ooh, don't trip, Tee. I'ma serve y'all, but for now I submit—y'all win."

Tasha and Nicole looked at each other and back at Billie who was now holding his hands in the air.

"No bullshit, tonight I'm done. You and Tee win."

Tasha and Nicole high-fived each other laughed.

"Yeah, have y'all fun, it'll be my turn soon."

Tasha rolled her eyes. "Nigga, whatever, you always get us, so it should be nothing," she said, and crossed her arms across her chest.

"It isn't," Billie replied, smiling. "Now let's clean up our mess and get some sleep. We have a big day tomorrow plus," he said with a smirk, "y'all gotta get up a little early to do y'all hair," Billie said, and ran into the kitchen.

"Nigga, fuck you," they both yelled.

He began laughing as they followed him into the kitchen so they could help him clean up the mess they had made.

It took them forty-five minutes to finish cleaning up all the water on the floor in the kitchen. Billie, once done, sat in one of the chairs at the dining room table, drinking a glass of water, while Tasha wiped down the sliding glass doors.

"I'ma go get some sheets for your bed, Tee, and put this trashcan back in the bathroom. I'll be right back," Nicole said. She gave Billie a kiss and exited the kitchen.

Billie watched Nicole go down the hall taking the trashcan to the guest bedroom, and go up the stairs to get the sheets. Tasha was spraying Windex on the window when Billie came up behind her placing both hands on the windows blocking her in between him and the glass doors. He pressed his dick up against her ass.

"I'm getting tired of your smart ass mouth Tee," Billie whispered in her ear.

Tasha arched her ass against his dick. "Move," she moaned.

"Make me," Billie whispered in her ear, before sucking her earlobe.

Tasha slowly turned around, facing him.

"You get on my nerves," she told him, as she looked in his eyes. Her pussy was wet and throbbing feeling his dick up against her leg. "I hate—"

Billie began kissing Tasha, cutting her sentence off. Tasha moaned softly, as their tongues danced. Billie took one of his hands off the glass door and grabbed Tasha's ass. Tasha dropped the towel and stuck her hand down the front of his sweat pants. She grabbed his dick, and broke their kiss.

"You make me so sick," she said seductively, as she slid down to a squatting position. Tasha pulled the front of his sweats down and put Billie's dick in her mouth.

'Ooh, Tee," Billie moaned, and looked toward the stairs to see if Nicole was coming.

Tasha began bobbing her head, sucking his dick, as if her life depended on it. Just as Billie's head fell back, enjoying Tasha's head game, she stopped, slowly pulled his dick out her mouth and stood up, looking him in his eyes again.

"That's what good boys get," Tasha said, and kissed him.

"Thank you for making time for me," she kissed him again. "Now move!"

Tasha pushed his chest, but Billie didn't budge. He stuck his hand down the front of her boy shorts and stuck his index finger in her pussy. Tasha moaned, and bit her bottom lip so she wouldn't get loud. Billie removed his finger from her pussy and his hand from her boy shorts. He stuck his finger in Tasha's mouth and she began sucking on it.

"You make me sick," Billie said, mocking her. He removed his index finger from her mouth, sucked it, walked over to the dining room table and sat down.

Tasha picked her towel back up and began cleaning the windows again.

"The feeling is mutual," she said, as she sprayed the window with Windex.

Nicole came down the stairs with the new comforter and sheet set for Tasha's bed just as Billie was taking a drink of water. Nicole set the comforter and sheets on the table.

"Okay, here are your replacements," she said, and sat on Billie's lap.

Nicole felt his dick and looked at him smiling. She wrapped her arms around his neck then whispered in his ear. "I got to get some of that later."

"I'ma hold you to that, Cola," Billie stated, and kissed her neck.

Tasha looked on jealously. *He supposed to be mine. I'm so fucken stupid*, she thought, as she slammed the bottle of Windex on the sink.

"I'ma go make my bed," she said, grabbing the stuff Nicole set on the table!

"Tee, what's wrong?" Nicole asked, grinding on Billie's lap.

"Nothing bitch, I'm PMS'ing," Tasha went down the hallway to the guest bedroom and started pulling the sheets off her bed.

Billie smacked Nicole on her ass. "Go help your friend," he said, and kissed her on the lips. "I'll be up stairs waiting on you, so you can keep your word."

Billie took the stairs two at a time, as Nicole went into the guest bedroom to help Tasha make the bed.

Nicole entered the guest bedroom, as Tasha was putting the new sheets on the bed. Tasha looked up.

"Hey Cola, I'm sorry for the way I acted in the kitchen, I was cramping," she lied, as Nicole helped her put the comforter on the bed.

"Girl don't trip, you know I understand. You want a Motrin," Nicole asked concern in her voice?

"Naw Bitch, it was gas. When I came in here, I cut one. I feel a whole lot better now."

They both started laughing.

"Ugh bitch, that's what that old cheese smell is," Nicole said, playfully while giggling.

"Naw bitch, that's yo funky ass breath."

They shared another laugh.

"Well, I'ma let you get some sleep okay. I love you," Nicole said, giving Tasha a hug.

"I love you too," Tasha replied, as they released each other.

"We gotta get up a little bit earlier so we can do our hair."

They shared another laugh.

"Yeah, because of yo nigga, all that time at Chuck's was for nothing," Tasha stated, while running her fingers through her hair then frowning, as her fingers got tingled. "He gets on my damn nerves," Tasha said, with attitude.

"Yeah, but tonight we got the last laugh," Nicole said, as she walked out the room pulling the door closed, still laughing. "I'll see you in the morning," Nicole left the door cracked, as she walked away.

Tasha sat on the end of the bed once Nicole left. She was shocked at how mad she'd gotten seeing Nicole sitting on Billie's lap.

"Damn, I'm falling in love with this nigga and getting jealous," Tasha said aloud, and thought for a moment. "Or was

I already in love the whole time and it's just now coming out?" She grabbed the remote, turning on the flat screen TV hanging on the wall in front of the bed.

"This shit is going to be harder than I thought," she started flicking threw the channels thinking about the kiss her and Billie shared in the kitchen and how good it felt when he grabbed her ass and stick his finger inside of her pussy. Tasha's pussy got wet, as she remembered him sucking her finger after she had sucked it first.

"God, please help me," Tasha said, feeling her pussy throbbing, as she decided to watch the Avengers. She reached over to the side of the bed, looked in her bag and grabbed her vibrator. Tasha placed it under her pillow still deep in thought.

"I'ma have to relieve some of this tension a little later," she said, patting the pillow, "Or a bitch going to go crazy.

*   *   *   *   *

Nicole made it up the stairs and laughed to herself, as she heard Billie cussing and yelling at Zane through his headset.

"Damn, Zane, why you ain't covering me? Why you blind? Nigga, shoot that bitch-ass muthafuckin' sniper on the roof! He's trying to kill me. I can't come from around this building to protect DeShawn. Nigga, kill that son of a bitch."

Nicole walked into the room and climb in the bed. She had planned to make love to Billie, but hearing him so into the game, she decided not to disturb him. Her head hit the goose feather pillow and she realized just how tired she was.

"Fuck that," she said, as she yawned, "he don't deserve no pussy anyway. He fucked up my hair, his ass on punishment." She started giggling to herself, as she pulled the comforter over her body. Nicole turned on her side with a smirk on her face thinking of how much fun she had this afternoon. She looked at the clock on her DVR, it was 10:45, and she was sound asleep by 10:47.

CHAPTER 19

Billie, Zane and DeShawn had completed six missions together since he had come up stairs. He was feeling good because his whole crew wasn't playing with them, but the three of them had done what the book to the game said would take a team of six to complete.

"Alright, y'all, we going to wrap it up for the night," Billie said, into his headset, as they cleared another mission.

"That's cool with me," Zane replied. "I'm tired."

"Yeah, me too. A nigga gonna grab something to eat and hop in the bed," DeShawn stated.

"Alright, bet. I'll get back with y'all tomorrow after the concert. If Anthony and Jamal get online, y'all try to get some missions completed so we can advance even further. Zane you Second Lt., make sure you keep this shit tight."

"Nigga, you know I got this shit," Zane stated, with confidence! "Have fun, my nigga."

"I'ma try!"

"Nigga, you taking fine ass Nicole and Tasha to a concert, how can you not have fun?" DeShawn asked, laughing.

"Shit, because they going to be screaming another nigga's name the whole time we there!"

All three of them started laughing.

"Yeah, ain't no fun hearing another nigga's name called," Zane said, still laughing.

"How true, how true," DeShawn stated, still laughing himself.

"I'm out. Y'all niggas stay safe." Billie turned off his PS3 and pulled off his headset. He was thirsty as a horse. He looked at the time on his Movado. "Damn, it's 1:30 AM in the morning, time be flying when a nigga playing that game."

He walked out his game room. He was about to go downstairs, but decided to check on Nicole first. She looked like an angel lying in bed fast asleep. Billie kissed Nicole on the forehead and headed out the room and down the stairs to the kitchen so he could get a Hawaiian Punch.

Billie was coming out the kitchen and headed back up the stairs when he heard a low humming sound coming from the guest bedroom. Billie looked down the hallway leading to the guest bedroom. The door was slightly open. *It's probably the TV*, Billie thought, as he took a drink of Hawaiian Punch and started up the stairs again. Once again, he stopped in his tracks, but this time it wasn't because of the humming sound, it was because he heard Tasha moaning.

I know this bitch ain't got no nigga in my house, Billie thought as his mind began to play tricks on him and he started getting jealous at the thought of someone else fucking Tasha. "Why do I care?" Billie said to himself, realizing that he had Nicole upstairs and couldn't expect Tasha not to get her needs met because they were creeping. He started back up the stairs; he was half way up when he heard Tasha moaning again, this time louder than before. He stopped moving so he could listen for a minute. All he could hear was Tasha's moans of pleasure. Curiosity got the best of him. He walked back down the stairs. He had made it up then went down the hallway that led to the guest bedroom. Billie could now hear the humming sound again. The closer he got to the door the louder the humming and moaning got. Billie didn't want to fuck with the door, just in case she did have company, but he had to push it open a little so he could see inside.

This bitch trying to piss me off, bringing a nigga in my house, he thought, as he put a little pressure on the door. He needed it to open a few more inches so he could see inside the room. The door opened without making a sound. Billie inhaled, he couldn't understand why her being with someone else had him so bent out of shape and he had Nicole. The truth was he wanted Tasha all to himself. He had always wanted Tasha, but was too scared in junior high to admit it.

He looked in the room; there wasn't a nigga in his house. Tasha was facing directly toward the door with her legs wide open, knees pulled back toward her shoulders. Her hand was between her legs, and she had what appeared to be a small vibrator in her hand. It was the size of a magic marker. Tasha was running it across her clit. Tasha's other hand was massaging her right breast. The way she was squeezing it made her nipple hard and made Billie want it in his mouth. Billie bit his lip to stifle a moan from escaping his mouth, as his eyes focused on Tasha's wet fat pussy.

This is too close to home, Billie thought. He wanted to back away from the door, but his feet wouldn't move. He adjusted his rock hard dick and turned around to walk away from the door, just as Tasha decided to change positions. Her movement caught his attention and he brought his face back to the crack in the door. Tasha turned over onto her knees and widened her stance, as she leaned forward, tooting her ass in the air. Tasha steadied herself on one elbow on the bed while she reached underneath her and continued to massage her clitoris with the vibrator. From this position, Billie could see every part of Tasha's sexuality; her beautiful full breast hung, which made her nipples even harder because now the blood flowed down into them. Tasha's asshole looked as if it was winking, as her muscles contracted from the pleasure that the vibrator was giving her clit. Tasha's fat wet pussy was the last thing that caught Billie's attention. It was more than beautiful; her pussy lips were small and pouting. It looked like a rose that hadn't fully bloomed. Billie's dick was standing straight out; it was harder than he could ever remember it being. Billie's dick began to think for him as Tasha let all her upper body weight rest on one shoulder while she inserted her middle finger into her tight wet pussy. She let out a low moan as it slid completely in. As she moved her finger in and out, Billie pushed the door all the way open. Tasha didn't stop when she heard the door open; she simply looked over her shoulder into Billie's eyes.

"Hmm Billie, come fuck me," she moaned.

Billie's mind went completely blank. He walked up behind Tasha, pulling down his pajama bottoms. Just as Tasha removed her finger from her pussy, Billie inserted his dick. Her pussy was so tight and wet that Billie couldn't help but moan her name as her pussy slowly received every inch of his ten-inch dick.

"Ooh Billie," Tasha moaned, "Fuck me nigga, *fuccccck…*"

Billie began ramming in and out of Tasha, which cut her demands short. The sensation Tasha was feeling was driving her insane. The lips of her pussy held tightly on to Billie's dick. Tasha was rocking back and forward to meet each one of Billie's thrust.

"Ooooh God, uuuummm," Tasha moaned as Billie began pumping faster.

"I'm coming Tee, bitch I'm uuuugh…" Billie released his load all inside of Tasha.

Tasha's body began to shake wildly; she bent down into the pillow as she found her own climax. Billie was still thrusting as Tasha screamed loudly into the pillow as her body went completely sluggish. Billie pulled his now limp dick out of her pussy. Tasha's walls held tightly to his dick not wanting to let him go. Tasha couldn't move. She still had her face in the pillow trying to catch her breath. Billie pulled up his pajama pants breathing hard and walked out the guest bedroom closing the door behind him. Tasha laid there unable to move. She fell asleep just how Billie had left her, ass in the air and face in the pillow.

Billie crawled into the bed next to Nicole. He lay on his back still trying to catch his breath. In his whole life, he never could remember losing control of himself as he did tonight. He looked over at Nicole whom was still sound asleep. He loved Nicole. There was no doubt in his mind about that, but Tasha made him feel a way that Nicole never had. When he was inside of Tasha, he felt like his dick belonged there.

"I'm tripping it's just lust," he told himself, as Nicole turned over opened her eyes and looked at him. She moved closer to him then laid her head on his chest.

"How long you been in bed next to me?" she asked, wrapping her arms around him.

"For about forty-five minutes," he lied, now holding her.

Nicole kissed his chest. "I love you, Daddy!"

Billie exhaled then kissed her on the top of her head. "I love you too," Billie replied, as he noticed her breathing change. "I love you too, Cola!"

Billie held Nicole tightly while she slept trying to figure out what he was going to do about Tasha. As he fell asleep, he realized he might have bitten off more than he could chew.

Nicole woke up at about 7:34 AM on Sunday morning. Billie was still sleeping, as she slid out his embrace. Nicole lightly kissed his lips and pulled the covers over him, as she got out the bed. Nicole knew it would take her and Tasha at least two hours to re-do their hair, so she decided that they needed to get started now if they wanted to get to the concert early. Nicole figured she'd let Billie sleep while her and Tasha did their hair. She would wake him after they finished and were making breakfast. She also planned to get a quickie before they left. Nicole giggled to herself, as she descended the stairs. She went down the hallway and entered the guest bedroom. Nicole started laughing as she closed the door behind her. Tasha's head was in the pillow, her ass was in the air and a vibrator lay on the floor still humming.

"Bitch wake yo nasty ass up," Nicole said, still laughing.

Tasha let out a soft moan, but didn't move.

Nicole continued laughing.

"You so damn nasty, bitch. What you do, wore yo'self out last night?" Nicole asked, slapping Tasha on the ass. "Get yo ass up!"

Tasha rolled on her side.

"What time is it?" she asked in a lazy voice.

"Almost 8:00 AM, you know we need to do our hair. Damn, I see you enjoyed yourself last night," Nicole stated, as she picked up the vibrator and cut it off. But, I'm not mad at you. Shit, you ain't got a man, so you gotta get yours the best way you can."

Bitch if only you knew, Tasha said, getting up and walking to the bathroom, still naked.

Nicole noticed how Tasha was walking and giggled to herself. "Shit and from the way you walking this muthafucka ain't no joke! I'ma have to get me one of these," Nicole said, cutting it on again, then cutting it off and placing it back on the bed giggling.

Fed up with Nicole smart remarks gave, Tasha gave one of her own.

"Shit, what you need a toy for when you got a bull upstairs. Bitch I know he keep you walking funny."

Nicole laughed. "Bitch, whatever, but yeah, he does his stuff, but I ain't never woke up with my ass in the air and my face in a pillow," Nicole said, jokingly.

"Yo bad, because I have and it felt um, um, good," Tasha said, as she cut the water on so she could brush her teeth. Tasha finished brushing her teeth then washed her face and came out the bathroom. She picked up her vibrator then kissed it.

"Bitch you is so damn nasty," Nicole said, laughing.

Tasha winked at Nicole, and placed her toy under her pillow.

"Whatever Cola, I'll be nasty as long as I get mine and last night I got mine."

Nicole laughed. "Yeah I know, remember I'm the one who woke you up with yo ass still tooted in the air," Nicole said, giggling.

"If you only knew," Tasha said, as she put on her shorts and her wife-beater with a smile on her face. "Cola, if you only knew."

They went into the bathroom to get started on their hair with Tasha still smiling. Feeling she was missing something, Nicole looked at Tasha.

"Bitch, if I only knew what?"

Tasha laughed at Nicole's question. "How good it feels to go to sleep and wake up like I did," Tasha replied sarcastically.

"Bitch, you so damn nasty," Nicole said, as she plugged the curlers up and grabbed the pressing comb out the cabinet. They walked out the bathroom and headed toward the kitchen to put the pressing comb on the stove.

"Yeah, I'm a nasty bitch," Tasha said, with a devilish grin on her face, "but last night I got my fire put out."

They both started laughing.

"Yeah, I'ma have to get me one of those," Nicole said, cutting the stove on and placing the pressing comb on it.

"You have no idea," Tasha stated, once again as she took a seat at the kitchen table with a smirk on her face. "Bitch, you have no idea."

CHAPTER 20

BILLIE WOKE UP TO THE SMELL of bacon, eggs, sausage and grits. As he opened his eyes, he noticed two of the most beautiful women in southern Los Angeles standing over him.

"Good morning," he said, as Nicole placed the tray with his plate across his lap.

Tasha poured him a glass of orange juice, then sat it on his tray as well and smiled.

"What did I do to deserve this?" he asked, feeling like a king.

They smiled at him.

"This is just our way of saying thank you for the tickets and backstage passes. We appreciate you!"

Billie put a fork full of cheese eggs in his mouth and bit into a piece of sausage. "Well, you're welcome," he said, then smiled and all jokes aside, "Y'all's hair looks nice!"

That got a smile from Nicole and Tasha.

"Thank you," they said in unison.

Still smiling and chowing down, Billie said, "Naw, thank you!"

They laughed at him as he ate as if he was deprived of food and this was his first meal in weeks.

"Well, Daddy, we about to take our showers and get dressed," Nicole said, as she and Tasha started to leave the room.

"Okay," Billie replied. "As soon as I'm done eating, I'll shower and we can head out. What time is it?"

Tasha looked at her Tag Watch. "It's ten-thirty."

"Alright, y'all go get ready. I'll be done in a few minutes."

Nicole and Tasha went downstairs. "Girl, go ahead and take you shower, I'ma go take mine. I'll meet you back down here in forty-five minutes or so."

Tasha nodded in agreement.

"We need to hurry up if we want to get to the concert early," Nicole confirmed.

Tasha started walking down the hallway to the guest bedroom. "Bitch, I'll be ready in thirty minutes," she stated closing the door as Nicole ran back up the stairs trying to figure out how she was going to get in a quickie.

Billie had just finished his food. He was sitting his tray to the side getting out the bed when Nicole ran into their bedroom, closing the door with a grin on her face.

"What's wrong with you?" Billie asked, eyeing her.

Nicole began taking off her clothes, walking toward the bathroom.

"I was just wondering if you would like to take a shower with me," she asked, seductively, throwing her clothes at him as she entered the bathroom.

Billie laughed as he heard the water turning on. He took off his pajama bottoms and wife-beater. "What's a nigga to do," he said, to himself as he entered the bathroom seeing Nicole holding the shower door open for him, smiling.

"What's a nigga to do?" Billie grabbed Nicole's ass and pulled her close to him. They began kissing as the water hit their bodies.

Tasha took a quick shower then dried off. She picked up her overnight bag, reached into it grabbing her Bath & Body Works Kiwi Strawberry lotion and rubbed it over her body. Once she was finished, Tasha walked over to the closet and grabbed her Louis Vuitton outfit that was brought for the concert. She decided against wearing any panties or bra. It took her five minutes to get into her pants; they were so tight, they looked painted on. Tasha put on the top, fastening the four buttons. Her breast looked like they would pop out at any given minute, but looks could be deceiving, because the top help them firmly in place. Tasha put on her seven-inch heels and the belt that made her outfit look like it was a one piece instead of two. Tasha walked over to the mirror, did a 360-degree turn, and then smiled. "Damn, I look good," she stated, as she walked over to her overnight bag, reaching inside to grab her five-karat princess cut diamond heart-shaped earrings, her Tiffany & Company white gold chain with an eight karat heart pendant and her white gold six karat tennis bracelet. She went back to the mirror to put on her jewelry. She smiled at the image that looked back at her.

"You a bad bitch," Tasha said, pointing at her reflection. She opened the door to the guest bedroom, and headed into the living room. Once there she went to the entertainment system, put in Rick Ross's *Maybach Music* CD, turned to song #2, turned up the volume to sixteen and started singing along with Rick Ross as he let the world know his bitch was bad, looking like a bag of money.

*   *   *

Nicole was bent over holding on for dear life to the shower rail getting her pussy beat up from the back when she heard the music come on.

Nicole moaned as Billie held tightly to her hips, ramming his dick in and out of her. She felt him speed up and now he was about to cum. Nicole arched her back, now trying to match his thrust with her own.

"Ooh, Daddy, ooh shit, nigga, I'ma cum, I…" Nicole moaned as he called her name, about to nut himself.

Their knees buckled as they came together, moaning each other's name.

Nicole stood upright, then turned around and kissed Billie as the water hit his back. "I love you, Daddy," she said, then nibbled on his bottom lip.

"I love you, too," Billie moaned, then squeezed her ass. "Now get out of the shower with me and get dressed so we can get out of here before you start something else and we won't be going anywhere," Billie said, opening the shower door.

Nicole kissed him again. "Okay, Daddy, but later on after the concert, you gotta break me off a piece of that Kit Kat bar."

Billie laughed, and then smacked her on the ass. "If you don't get your horny ass out of this bathroom, I'ma break you off more than a piece," he said, laughing as his dick began to get hard again.

Nicole giggled, grabbed a towel and then ran out the bathroom, laughing when she saw his little man getting ready for round two. "Daddy, I ain't fucking with you …"

Billie laughed, closing the shower door. "Yeah," he yelled, as he let the water hit his chest. "Because if you do, there's going to be three empty front row seats, because you know round two is always an hour or better."

Nicole laughed from the bedroom. "Yeah and Tee would kill us both if we make her miss Trey Songz."

Billie's dick stood up at the mentioning of Tasha's name. As he turned off the water, he grabbed a towel and began drying off as he walked out the bathroom.

Nicole had just finished putting on lotion. She looked up to see Billie's dick sticking straight out toward her.

A devilish smirk came across her face. "But there's nothing wrong with me giving you a little head real fast," she said, as she dropped to her knees and took Billie's dick in her mouth. Billie moaned as Nicole began bobbing her head on his dick.

His last complete sentence before filling Nicole's stomach with his seed was, "Fuck, Trey Songz."

It took Nicole ten minutes to get inside her cat suit. It was so tight that there was no way anything could be worn up under, so she didn't try to put on a bra or panties. The suit looked like it was her skin. The only reason you knew it wasn't was because of the Louis Vuitton symbols that was all over it. You could see every curve on Nicole's body and in this suit; one could see why her nickname was Cola. Nicole put on her seven-inch Louis Vuitton heels and placed her six karat platinum princess cut diamond earrings in her ears. Nicole looked in her dresser and pulled out her platinum eight-karat tennis bracelet and her Tiffany & Company platinum chain with the eight-karat heart pendant. After placing them on, she went into the bathroom and sprayed on some Chanel Sexy perfume then looked in the mirror and smiled. She walked back in the bedroom; did a 360-degree turn in front of Billie.

"How do I look?"

Billie was speechless for a second. "Goddamn!" He finally was able to say after he found his voice and finished buttoning up his shirt. "I don't know if I want you to wear that." His mouth began to water as his dick throbbed in his pants. "You going to make me have to kill a nigga tonight."

Nicole laughed, then walked over and kissed him. "Shut up, Daddy," she said giggling as he squeezed her ass.

Nicole walked over to their bedroom door with Billie's eyes glued to her every move.

"I'ma go keep Tasha company, Daddy," Nicole said, seductively, looking over her shoulder at him. She blew him a kiss then closed the door behind her, leaving Billie speechless and with a hard dick.

Billie finally finished getting dressed. He'd changed outfits four times before deciding on a pair of True Religion denim jeans with the button down shirt to match, his Air Jordan III Retro's and since they were going to be out late, he grabbed his raw denim Motorcycle Jacket. He put on his Fegaro gold chain with the ten karat diamond cross and his Rolex. He sprayed on some Issey Miyake then headed down the stairs ready to leave.

"Take it to the Head," by Rick Ross, Nicki Minaj, Lil' Wayne and Trey Songz was banging throughout the house. As Billie got to the bottom of the stairs, he almost passed out from the loss of blood that went from his brain to his dick as he watched Nicole and Tasha dancing to the beat of the music. His mouth fell open as Tasha swayed her hips and made her ass jiggle; while Nicole popped her hips, making her ass bounce.

"Damn," he said louder than he meant to, making both of them stop dancing and look toward him. They giggled like a couple of schoolgirls.

"What! We was only dancing, Daddy," Nicole said, shyly, as she and Tasha looked Billie over.

Billie, now realizing he spoke out loud, laughed. "Naw, both of you look really nice, that's all," he said, as he stuck his hand in his pocket to adjust his dick before they noticed it was hard.

"Thank you," Nicole and Tasha said simultaneously, smiling.

Tasha, whose pussy was now wet, bit her bottom lip. "You look nice yourself," she said, then walked over to the sofa to grab her purse so that she wouldn't get caught by Nicole lusting over her man.

"Girl you ain't never lied," Nicole said, walking over to Billie giving him a kiss. "And, bitch he smells good, too," Nicole said, with a giggle.

Tasha sucked her teeth. "Bitch don't pump his head up too damn much," Tasha stated; that jealous feeling starting to flame up in her again. "Because you know we will have to deflate his ass!"

They all started laughing.

"Tee, why you hating on a nigga?" Billie asked, with a smirk on his face, grabbing his car keys.

"I'ma keep it One-Hundred, all bullshit and jokes to the side, both of you look too damn good. Shit, to be honest, there's not a word to describe how y'all look right now. I want to say beautiful, but you are beyond that. On my Momma, I'ma bring my gun, because a nigga fo' sho going to have to pop a nigga over y'all!"

Nicole and Tasha laughed.

"Whatever, Billie," Tasha said, as they walked out the front door and down the walkway to the car.

"Thank you, Daddy," Billie heard Nicole say as he locked the door, and then watched their asses as he walked behind them.

Yeah, he said, to himself, as his dick throbbed through his jeans. *A nigga gonna end up killing a motherfucker today.* He laughed to himself as he unlocked the doors for them to get in. Nicole blew him a kiss over the top of the car as she got in, while Tasha gave him a sexy wink.

What's a nigga to do? he thought as he got in the driver's seat, closed the door and started the Jag. *What's a nigga to do?* It was 12:40 PM, when they pulled off.

CHAPTER 21

THE CONCERT WAS OFF THE CHAIN. Nicole and Tasha loved every minute of it, even Billie had to admit it was way better than he expected. Tasha and Nicole had the time of their lives. They got attention not only from men and women who came to the concert, but also from the performers. Trey Songz, while singing, "Jupiter Love," grabbed Nicole's hand and tried to pull her on stage, which got Billie hot as fish grease, but when Nicole didn't let him pull her up to the stage, he let her go and winked at her, then grabbed Tasha's hand. When Tasha felt him pulling her toward him and on stage, she gladly went without any hesitation.

Billie, while watching Tasha on the stage, began to get hot around the collar. He began mad dogging Trey Songz, cussing under his breath. Nicole giggled as Trey Songz sung to Tasha as she danced for him, while looking into his eyes. Billie knew

Trey Songz was loving the way Tasha moved and worked her hips and ass, because his own dick was hard from just watching her on stage. After the song, Trey Songz gave Tasha a hug and asked the crowd to give Tasha a hand, which they did as he helped her off the stage.

Billie grabbed Tasha's available hand as she came down. Trey Songz and Billie made eye contact, and then gave each other a head nod in show of respect. Nicole and Tasha went crazy, talking about how Trey Songz was singing to them and how he was looking at them.

Blah, blah, blah, yada, yada, yada, etc., etc., etc., was all Billie heard as Lil'' Wayne came out with eight breathtaking women that damn hear didn't have on any clothes and was popping their asses to his hit song, "Every Girl in the World." Seeing Drake and Wayne on stage pumped Nicole and Tasha up even more. It got worse when Lil' Wayne said, "And we like and she likes us, too," and he pointed at Nicole and Tasha.

Billie laughed to himself, knowing he had two bad bitches with him. After the concert was over, they all went back stage. Billie, Nicole and Tasha got mad love and was able to take pictures with Lil' Wayne, Trey Songz, Drake, 2 Chains and Rick Ross. Billie stood in on a few of the pictures with them, but for the most part, he let them have their moment and enjoy themselves. When Nicki Minaj came up on the side of Billie while Nicole and Tasha were taking a photo with Drake, Billie almost lost his mind.

"Hey sexy," Nicki said, while smiling.

Billie, at a loss for words for a moment, just looked at her, and then catching himself, he moaned "Hi" so low that it made Nicki giggle.

Hearing her giggle made him laugh.

"I'm sorry," he stated regaining his composer. "But you're beautiful," Billie told her as he took in her whole body up close and not from a video or magazine.

"Thank you," Nicki responded, now looking him up and down. "But don't get it twisted you fine as hell, yo damn self."

That boosted Billie's confidence level 150%; his head was now about to float off his shoulders. He smiled and Nicki put her hand on his chest.

"Damn, you have a beautiful smile. Ooh, a bitch need that," Nicki said, now snapping her fingers at one of the photographers.

"Need what," Billie asked, as he felt her soft hand grab his.

"I need that picture taken with you," Nicki said, now smiling.

Nicki Minaj and Billie took seven photos together, four of them Nicki was so close to him that she could feel his dick.

"Oh and you packing, too," Nicki said, as she made one of her signature poses.

Nicole and Tasha were not done taking their photos and both were getting upset and jealous at how Nicki Minaj was popping her ass on Billie's dick, which made Nicole damn near run over and sock Nicki in her face. Tasha had to grab Nicole to keep her from reacting.

"That bitch need to stay in her lane," Nicole said through clench teeth, shooting daggers at Nicki Minaj as she hugged Billie and kissed him on the cheek.

"It was nice meeting you," Nicki said, then handed Billie a copy of the seven photos.

Nicki looked at Nicole and Tasha. "You need to keep a leash on him, because he so fine a bitch will try to steal him if given a chance."

Billie laughed, now loving the attention he was getting from a superstar.

Nicole rolled her eyes. "He ain't going nowhere," she stated with attitude, ready to whip Nicki's ass.

Tasha was ready to punch on Nicki; all she needed was a reason.

Nicki sized Tasha up as she walked away.

Nicki looked at Billie then winked. "I don't know about all that," Nicki said, sarcastically, then growled. "Like I said, keep a leash on him!" Nicki Minaj walked away giving Billie a real show as her ass switched from left to right.

Nicole and Tasha sucked their teeth and socked Billie at the same time.

"Ah, what the fuck was that for?" he asked, laughing while rubbing his arm.

"For being all up in that bitch's face like you single, nigga," Nicole said, frowning at him.

"Yeah, don't be disrespecting my girl in public like that," Tasha stated, with attitude. "That bitch's ass is fake anyway!"

Billie laughed. "It don't look fake to me!"

They hit him again.

"Okay, okay," Billie said, laughing. "It's funny how y'all was all up in them nigga's faces taking pictures and smiling and shit, but y'all wanna trip on me because I took a few pictures," Billie said, now looking at both of them.

Nicole looked in his eyes and then kissed him. "It's different, Daddy," she said, and then stepped back. "See I just took a few pictures standing next to those guys, but that bitch was all over you like a cheap suit."

Billie laughed. "Cola, please. Them niggas and I don't care what you say, they want to fuck both you and Tee. If I wasn't standing there and they thought y'all was alone, they would have tried to get y'all in that Hummer limo," Billie stated, now getting heated at them trying to make it like what they did was different from what he did.

"See, Daddy, that's just it, you right, they would have tried if you wasn't here, but out of respect for you they didn't and because I love you, I wouldn't let them nor would I have left with them because I love you. Now that snake bitch didn't give a fuck that we was standing there. She didn't have any respect for us at all that's why she was all over you like that. She was really just being a bitch, because she knew you was with us and seen us taking photos with Lil' Wayne and his crew."

Tasha nodded her head in agreement. "See, bitches do shit just to hate," Tasha stated.

Billie laughed. "Y'all bitches crazy as fuck." He grabbed their hands. "Come on, lets' get out of here."

"Yeah, lets' go," Nicole and Tasha said together. "Before Nicki Minaj gets a real Compton ass whipping," Nicole added.

They all laughed as they walked out the exit doors headed to Billie's Jag.

Billie, Nicole and Tasha pulled out of the parking lot of the Forum heading to the after party at the Valet Room in Malibu. Nicole was drunk and dozing off as they got on the Freeway. Tasha however being able to hold her liquor was awake and watching Billie through the rearview mirror.

"I think we should go home," Tasha said, noticing Nicole now passed out snoring in the passenger seat.

Billie looked over at Nicole. "Yeah, I think you're right. We ain't going to be able to enjoy ourselves at the after party with Cola being faded and you know how she gets when she's drunk, her ass will be passed out in the VIP booth and we will need to babysit her all night."

They laughed.

"Nicole knows she can't handle no liquor," Tasha stated, now smiling.

"Yeah, but that don't stop her from drinking."

Billie hit the 405 and headed home.

"Well at least you both enjoyed y'all selves. Shit, and you was really on stage grinding on your boy Trey Songz," Billie said, with a smirk.

"Did I make you jealous?" Tasha asked now staring at him through the rear view mirror. Her hazel eyes seemed to be looking right through him.

Billie looked over at Nicole whom was still snoring. "Naw, I'm not a hater," Billie stated, but in his heart, he had been jealous.

"Well just so you know I was thinking of you and watching you while I was up there," Tasha stated as she took her seat belt off and slid to the middle of the back seat. Tasha was buzzing, she was horny and her pussy was throbbing and soaking wet.

"Whatever, Tee." Billie said, with a laugh. "I was the furthest thing from your mind," Billie stated now exiting the 405, headed down La Tijera.

Tasha stuck her head between the driver and passenger seat. "You've been on my mind since the sixth grade, Billie," Tasha said, seductively as Billie stopped at the light on La Cienega.

He turned his head, looking into Tasha's eyes. "You so full of shi—"

Tasha stopped his statement with a kiss, their tongues danced in each other's mouths as Billie began running one of his hands over her breast. Tasha loved the way his hand felt on her body. Tasha broke the kiss, sucked and bit her bottom lip lightly as a car behind them blew its horn.

They both looked over at Nicole who was still knocked out cold. Billie turned on to La Cienega, heading toward home. His dick was now rock hard.

"You know how I feel about you, Billie," Tasha said, as Billie turned on Alvern. He pushed a button on his console. While turning into his driveway, the garage door slowly opened. He pulled into the garage then hit the button once again, closing the door.

Billie turned his head now looking straight into Tasha's beautiful hazel eyes. "I know how I feel, but this right here is a little too close for comfort," he said, then looked over at Nicole.

Tasha looked into his eyes, and then smiled. "You're right." Tasha slid back into the backseat then over to the left side passenger door opening it and got out closing it behind her.

"Go and get Nicole to bed," Tasha said, as she walked by the driver's side door looking at Billie. "Then once you do that come make some time to see about me." She walked into the house leaving Billie in the car watching her ass, while he held his dick.

Billie got Nicole out the car and carried her up the stairs into their bedroom. He pulled her shoes off her feet then pulled the covers over her and kissed her.

"Yo ass really don't need to drink," he said, then laughed as Nicole moaned and continued to snore.

Billie took off his jacket and hung it in the closet. He then took off his clothes, threw them in the cleaner bag and put on his pajama pants with a wife-beater.

"Come see about me," Billie said to himself, as he thought about Tasha, which made his dick hard. "This bitch bold as fuck," Billie stated, laughing to himself. Just as he was about to get into bed, Tasha was standing in his and Nicole's doorway in a sheer nightie with nothing under it. She was watching his every move while rubbing her pussy.

Billie nearly fell trying to get to the door before Nicole woke up to see Tasha doing what she was doing.

Billie closed the door as he pulled Tasha into the hallway.

"Tee, what the fuck you doing?" Billie asked with anger in his voice. "Bitch, you know motherfuckin' well you way out of line right now and if Nicole had woke up and seen you there she'd kill both of us!"

Tasha gave a devilish grin. "I told you to come see about me," she said, the smell of Remy strongly on her breath. "You was taking too damn long, so I came to see about you and as far as Cola is concerned, her ass is out for the night, trust me on that, plus she told me her home is my home; so, I'm making myself at home!"

Billie looked Tasha up and down; his dick was standing out like a flagpole. "Yo ass drunk, Tee. I'ma take you downstairs, you trippin'." Billie grabbed her arm, but Tasha pulled away.

"I'm not drunk, nigga," she said, loudly, which made Billie look at his bedroom door. "A little tipsy, but not drunk!"

"Okay, Tee," Billie said, now walking down the stairs hoping Tasha would follow. He didn't want Nicole waking up to this. It would be way too much he would have to explain. Tasha followed him down the stairs still talking shit.

"All you had to do was bring your stankin' ass down here and I wouldn't have had to come get you," Tasha said, now at the end of the stairs. They turned the corner with Billie facing her looking over his shoulder as he walked backwards toward the guest bedroom making sure he didn't run into anything.

"You right, Tee," Billie said, now entering the guest bedroom, still walking backwards.

Once Tasha was in the room, he walked forward closed the door and locked it. He noticed the Remy bottle on the dresser and knew if he picked it up it would damn near be empty.

"You damn right, I'm right," Tasha said, wrapping her arms around Billie's neck. "Nigga, did you know I wanted you to be mine first?" Tasha said, looking in his eyes.

Billie amazed by her statement just looked in her eyes at a loss for words.

"Yeah, I wanted you to be the first nigga to hit this pussy," Tasha said, then kissed his lips. "But yo punk ass wanted Nicole!"

Billie looked at Tasha as a tear fell down her face.

"Tasha, don't cry," Billie said, as he wiped the tears away. He kissed her lips, which made Tasha moan softly. "I told you I wanted you then, too."

Tasha ran her hand under his wife-beater then down his pajama bottoms and grabbed his dick.

"What about now?" Tasha asked, and then ran her tongue across her lips.

"Tee, I never stopped wanting you," Billie said, watching Tasha slowly slid down to her knees.

As Tasha placed Billie's dick in her mouth, he let out a moan of pleasure. Tasha bobbed her head making loud slurping sounds as she sucked his dick. Tasha stood back up then clawed on to the bed.

"Come show me," Tasha said, now letting Billie get an eye full of her beautiful perfectly round ass.

Billie pulled off his pajama pants as Tasha arched her ass in the air.

"Show me!"

Billie entered Tasha's wet tight pussy from the back. Tasha threw her pussy at him meeting his every thrust.

"Fuck me hard, Billie," Tasha moaned.

Billie grabbed her hips tighter and was now slamming into her so hard that he felt like his dick might get lost inside of her stomach.

"Ooh, fuck," Tasha screamed as she felt herself about to cum.

"Oooooh, Daddy, fuck me, B-I-L-L-I-E, oooh God, ooooh B-I-L-L-I-E, I'm about to cum," Tasha yelled then felt her legs giving in from up under her as her body began to shake uncontrollably.

Billie, still hard as steel, rolled her on her back, placed her legs on his shoulders and finished writing his name in Tasha's pussy. Tasha moaned in ecstasy as she stared at Billie while he hammered his dick in and out of her. Billie let out a moan of his own as he came so hard inside of Tasha that his knees buckled. Billie pumped a few more times making sure he'd made his point as he pulled his dick out of Tasha. She moaned, then bit her bottom lip, as he turned her over on her stomach then stuck a pillow under her stomach. Tasha screamed Billie's name out in both pain and pleasure as she felt the biggest dick in her life enter her ass. She arched her ass in the air then bit into the pillow as Billie hit her ass making his mark and claiming what was now for sure his. Tasha moaned into the pillow loving the way his dick felt inside her ass. Tasha knew she would never walk the same again, as cum began running out of her pussy like water as she felt Billie hit her G-Spot. Tasha began screaming at the top of her lungs as she had the best and first orgasm from getting fucked in her ass.

Billie released his load inside of her then fell beside her on the bed unable to move and trying to catch his breath. Tasha slid close to him and laid her head on his chest, and within seconds, they had fallen asleep with satisfied smiles on their faces. Neither of them concerned with the fact that Nicole was upstairs sleeping and could wake up at any second and catch them.

Billie woke up in his guest bedroom with Tasha wrapped in his arms. "Oh shit," he said out loud, realizing what had happened and that he had fallen asleep after he'd dicked Tasha down. "A nigga really slippin'," he said, as he got out of bed, waking Tasha up with his sudden movement.

"Umm, where you going?" Tasha moaned, reaching for him.

"Tee, we really trippin'," Billie said, pulling away from her, grabbing his pajama pants off the floor and putting them on.

Tasha, snapping back to reality, looked at the wall clock then jumped up herself. "OMG! I'm so sorry," Tasha stated, getting dressed, as Billie peeked out the door.

"It's cool, just pray Nicole didn't come down here and see us all hugged up while we was naked and asleep."

Tasha laughed. "Nigga, if that had happen, we both would be dead."

Billie slid out the room then laughed. "Yeah, you're right. I will see you later, Tee," he stated as he ran down the hallway and up the stairs.

Tasha stood in the doorway watching him. *You sure in the fuck will see me later*, she thought and then giggled. *Damn, I'm in love with my best friend's man.* Tasha shook her head as she closed the door and headed to the bathroom to take a shower. It was 9:40 AM when she turned the water on, smiling from ear-to-ear.

Once upstairs, Billie took a quick shower and slid in the bed. He looked over at Nicole who was still asleep. She was no longer snoring and now looked like an angel. Billie pulled the cover over her and kissed her cheek.

"I'm a fuckin' tramp," he said to himself, feeling guilty as he thought about what he had just done.

Billie laid there on his side trying to figure out how he had let all this happen. He last thought, before he dozed off to sleep, was that he was going to let his little head get him in a lot of trouble if he kept letting it think for the both of them. Billie fell asleep on top of the covers with Nicole tucked warmly underneath them next to him.

CHAPTER 22

MONICA WENT TO THE DOCTOR FOR a check-up and like her mother told her, she was pregnant. She was overjoyed to be having a baby on the way and couldn't wait to tell Billie about it. She had decided on telling him on their trip to Cancun. She knew that would be the perfect time, plus he would be all hers for a whole week; there would be no Nicole, no leaving to go home to the next bitch and no work. Just all play all her way. Monica laughed, as she thought of all the nasty ways she wanted to play with Billie, as she filed some papers.

Monica was in a good mood. Billie had called earlier and told her he would be spending the weekend with her. He informed her that Nicole and Tasha had a job convention in Palm Springs and that they wouldn't be back until Monday. Monica's pussy

234 | *Billie Dureyea Shell*

had been throbbing all day since she received that call from him; thinking about the pounding he was going to put on her pussy over the next few days had her soaking wet. Monica had been asking Billie questions about children over the last couple of weeks. The subject would always bring a smile to his face as he would go into detail on what kind of father he would be and how he would love to have a son and daughter, but he didn't think it would ever happed, because Nicole couldn't have children.

"Too bad; so sad for you, boo," Monica said, running her hand over her stomach. *I'ma give him what you can't and be the woman that he needs*, Monica thought as the phone rang. Monica answered the phone, took down the message and hung up, getting lost in her own thoughts once again. She smiled as she imagined Billie playing in the front year with their son while she watched them through the kitchen window, cooking dinner. Monica was pulled from her daydream as she heard Billie pulling up blasting, "Can You Stand the Rain" by New Edition on the car radio.

"Hell, yeah, I can stand the rain," Monica said, smiling as she ran to the back door to greet him.

As Billie got out of his Jag, Monica held the back door of the office open for him, smiling from ear to ear.

"Hey, boo," she greeted seductively, as he closed his car door grinning at her.

"If I didn't know any better, I'd think you missed me," Billie said, sarcastically.

Monica playfully hit him in the back of his head as he entered the door and she closed and locked it.

"I do miss you and you know it," Monica said, grabbing his shirt by the collar and kissing him. "And, I'ma show you just how much over the weekend," Monica said seductively.

In the past few weeks, Billie had been noticing that Monica had a shine about her. She was looking like she was glowing as well. Monica walked in front of him; he was now noticing that her ass, which was already perfect in every way, was filling out more and so was her hips.

Damn, he said to himself, as he watched her ass sway from left to right. Billie's dick began to get hard as Monica bent over to get him a cup from under the cabinet to pour him a glass of Simply Social pink lemonade. Her very low cut skirt revealed that she didn't have on any panties; it also showed him all her assets. Billie's dick damn hear jumped out of his zipper as Monica looked over her shoulder and into in eyes.

"Do you like what you see?" Monica asked, then bit her bottom lip and shook her ass.

Billie walked up behind her, unzipped his pants, his dick jumping out as soon as his zipper was down which made Monica giggle.

"I guess that answers my question," she said, as he grabbed her hips.

Monica moaned loudly as Billie entered her. She grabbed the side of the cabinet as he slowly began to bring his dick in and out of her. Monica's pussy felt like an oven, it was so warm and tight that Billie couldn't even think straight.

"Oow shit, Monica," he moaned as he felt her working her hips and ass as he slid all the way in her. Monica arched her back and began bouncing her ass against his thighs as he thrust in and out of her.

"Oh, Daddy, fuck me. Yes, Billie, hit this pussy. Emmm, it's yours. Ow my God, it's all yours," Monica screamed in ecstasy as his dick filled her up.

Monica felt herself about to have an orgasm and began working her pussy muscles making her pussy even tighter.

"Ooh fuck, you got some good ass pussy," Billie said between clinch teeth, now pounding hard and fast into her, not able to control himself anymore.

Monica screamed as her knees buckled and she was coming hard, losing control of her body.

Billie placed his arm under Monica's stomach, holding her up as she violently began to shaking.

"Fuck," she yelled as thick white cream began oozing out of her pussy and down Billie's balls. Monica regained her balance and Billie pulled his dick out of her, which made Monica's eyes roll to the back of her head.

He turned her around and sat her on top of the cabinet. They began kissing and he pulled the front of her shirt open, her bra unclipped in the front, which made Billie smile. He unleashed her breast and was speechless at how much fuller and beautiful they looked. He took her nipples one at a time in his mouth making Monica gasp. She moaned, loving the way his tongue and mouth felt on her breast.

"I love you," Monica moaned as Billie grabbed her ass, sitting her on top of his dick. Monica wrapped her arms around his neck and her legs around his waist as he brought her up and down on his dick.

"Ooh my God, Billie, I love you. Mmmm I looovvve you," she moaned. Monica let her head fall back feeling herself about to cum again. Billie began bringing her up and down faster and faster.

"Ooh Monica, ooh shit, I love you, too," he moaned.

Monica, hearing him say those words, began crying as a gut wrenching orgasm took over her body. Monica held on tightly as Billie released his seed inside of her. Billie kissed Monica's neck while she held on to him, not wanting to let go. After relieving himself, Billie sat Monica on the cabinet, removing his now limp dick from inside of her. Monica looked into his eyes and kissed him.

"I really love you, Billie," Monica said sincerely, as tears fell from her eyes.

Billie kissed her lips and wiped away her tears. "Mo, I love you, too, please don't cry. Did I hurt you?" he asked, with concern in his voice.

Monica grabbed Billie, holding him close to her. "No baby," she said, kissing him on the cheek. "You just made me the happiest woman in the world!"

Billie gave her a kiss as he pulled away from her. "Why, what did I do?" he asked, smiling which made Monica's pussy twitch.

"Being you and letting me know you love me, that's what you did," Monica replied, now smiling back at him. "And, there's something I need to tell you," she stated now wrapping her arms around his neck as he held her around her waist.

"What is it, Mo?" Billie asked with curiosity in his eyes.

"I was going to wait 'til we got to Cancun, but now is the perfect time. Billie, I'm going to have your baby. I'm pregnant!"

Billie's mouth flew open. He looked at Monica in a daze, which made her start crying.

"I'm sorry," she said, feeling she had made him mad and told him too soon.

Billie snapped out of his daze; hearing her crying again and smiled. "What's wrong now?" Billie asked, kissing her tears.

"You mad at me because I'm pregnant and I...I...I—"

Billie kissed her, cutting off her sentence. "I'm not mad at you, Monica," Billie stated, smiling again at her. "I was just shocked that's all. I can't explain the feeling I got when you told me you was going to have my baby, but I felt wonderful."

Monica's face lit up. "You're happy?" Monica asked, now smiling.

"Yeah, of course, I'm happy. This will be my first child!"

Monica kissed him. "Ooh, thank you for not being mad at me. I love you so much!"

Billie looked at her seriously. "I love you, too, Mo; but, I'm going to ask you a question," he said, which got Monica's full attention. "What the fuck we going to do, keep this under wraps, because we can't let Nicole know?"

Monica's words flew out her mouth before she could stop them. "What the fuck you mean, we can't let her know? I'm about to have our baby!" Monica looked at him angrily.

"That's just it, Mo. You are about to have our child, but how do we explain how the fuck that came about?" Billie asked looking into her eyes. "How the fuck do I explain to a woman that I love and live with that I got another woman, my secretary, that I love as well, pregnant?" he asked her, looking for an answer in her eyes.

Monica kissed him on the lips. "You don't try, Daddy, you do like Nike say!"

Billie zipped up his pants then walked over to his desk. "Monica it's not that easy," he said, sitting down in his chair, now thinking to himself that he should HAVE used a condom, but he did want a child and Nicole couldn't give him one, but that still didn't make what he did okay, nor any easier to except.

"Damn," Billie stated as he looked up at the ceiling, lost in thought.

Monica walked over to the front of the desk then looked him in the eyes. "Well, you're going to have to figure out something, because we about to bring a child into this world and me and our baby are going to need you," Monica stated with conviction.

"I know this, I just gotta figure out how the fuck I'ma work this out," Billie replied, knowing that he had just bit off way more than he could chew.

"Don't worry, we will figure it out together," Monica said, as she sat on his lap, placing his hand on her stomach."

Billie rubbed her stomach, shaking his head. *What's a nigga to do?* he thought, as a smile came across his face at the vision of playing catch with his son ran through his mind.

"What the fuck is a nigga to do?" He closed his eyes, still rubbing Monica's stomach, wondering what had he gotten himself into.

*   *   *

Nicole and Tasha shared a President Suite in the Palm Springs resort on the seventh floor. Their room looked more like an apartment instead of a hotel room. It had a seventy-two-inch flat screen in the living room with a leather sofa and love seat. There was a Jacuzzi and kitchen and a dining room. It even had a fully loaded mini bar. The two large bedrooms that were very tastefully furnished had fifty-two-inch TVs on the walls. Both rooms also had a California king-sized waterbeds. Nicole and

Tasha could see why the rooms cost $225.00 a night and was glad their jobs were paying for it.

Tasha had been running back and forth to the bathroom all day throwing up.

"Bitch, it's probably the change in the air," Nicole said, as she cooked Tasha some chicken noodle soup. "Because you know the air is way cleaner up here, less pollution than in Los Angeles."

Tasha came out the bedroom. "Girl, I don't know what the hell is wrong with me, it's like my senses are more acute than normal and if I smell something I don't like my stomach does flips and I have to throw up," Tasha said, walking into the kitchen.

"Well, if you keep feeling this way, we going to have to get you to a doctor," Nicole said, sitting the bowl of soup on the table with a bottle of cranberry juice. "But, for now come eat this soup I made for you, it should settle your stomach!"

Tasha sat at the table and began eating the soup and crackers; her stomach didn't react to it, so she finished the bowl.

"So you just gotta bug that's all," Nicole said, picking up the empty bowl and placing it in the dishwasher.

Tasha downed her juice then got up to throw the container in the trash. "I guess you're right, it's just a bug," Tasha stated, as she began walking toward her room. "I'm going to go lay down. Thank you for the soup. Wake me up in a few hours, don't let me sleep all day," Tasha said, as she was about to walk into her room.

"Okay, but holla if you need me," Nicole stated looking at Tasha, worried about her best friend.

Just as Tasha was about to lay down her stomach turned. She put her hand over her mouth and ran out the room for the bathroom. Nicole was on her heels as Tasha fell on the floor, hugging the toilet with her head in it. Nicole pulled Tasha's hair back as she threw up for the fourth time that day.

"Okay, now we're going to the doctor," Nicole said, rubbing Tasha's back lovingly. "We can't be having this shit." Nicole closed her eyes, saying a silent prayerm hoping her girl was okay.

*   *   *

Billie was lying on his back getting his balls and dick sucked when his cell phone began ringing. He grabbed it off the dresser next to Monica's bed as Monica began deep throating him causing him to almost drop the phone.

"Damn, Mo," Billie moaned, as he looked at his cell phone screen to see who was calling. "Shit," he stated between moans as he answered the phone on the forth ring, trying to stop Monica from sucking his dick by slowly removing it out of her mouth so he could talk.

Monica sucked her teeth then came up to lay beside him with an attitude as he said, "Hello!"

"Hey, Daddy," Nicole said, hearing her man's voice. "How are you doing?"

"I'm fine," Billie replied, as Monica began sucking on his chest and running her tongue down his stomach. "How are you and Tee doing?" he asked, as Monica ran her tongue back up his body and started placing soft kisses on his neck.

"Well, I'm okay, but Tee been sick since we got here. We at the hospital now; she been throwing up all day."

Billie exhaled in the phone as Monica began sucking his dick again.

"I hope she is okay," he stated trying to hold back a moan of pleasure as Monica bobbed her head on his dick.

"I hope so, too. We been here for an hour or so…," Nicole paused. "Daddy, what's that noise," Nicole asked, referring to the slurping sounds Monica was making while sucking his dick.

Billie placed his free hand on the back of Monica's head. "Fuck," he yelled as Monica began deep throating him.

"Daddy, it's going to be okay," Nicole said, thinking Billie was reacting and getting upset about Tee being sick.

"I know it will be okay. I'm sorry about the outburst and that noise is the TV," Billie lied as Monica took his dick out her mouth, cupped his balls in her hand and began sucking them.

"Ooh God, I hope Tasha is okay," Billie moaned as Monica ran her tongue from his balls to the head of his dick.

"She'll be fine, Daddy," Nicole replied. "I love you. Here comes the doctor, I'ma call you back, okay?"

"Okay," Billie moaned, "I love you too!" He hung up the phone then dropped it on the floor as Monica came up from sucking his dick and sat on it and began riding him.

"Next time that motherfucker ring and it's not yo momma, you better let it go to voice mail," Monica said slowly riding his dick.

"You know I can't just ignore Cola's calls like tha...ooh shit, Mo," Billie moaned as he felt her pussy walls tighten around his dick.

"Like I said, Daddy," Monica state seductively, now working her hips and moving up and down slowly with her hands placed on his chest as she looked in his eyes. "While you over here, on my time, the next time that phone rings it goes to voice mail, unless it's yo momma!"

Billie's eyes rolled in the back of his head as he moaned. "You got that, Mo," he said, placing his hands on her hips.

Monica smiled as she worked her hips and ass faster as she rode him. Monica knew how to work her pussy and was now doing just that. "Ummm hmmm, this your pussy, Billie," Monica moaned then began thrusting her hips harder to meet Billie's thrust.

"Damn, Mo. You got some good ass pussy," Billie stated, placing his hands on her ass helping her to go up and down on his dick.

"Ooh, Daddy, oooow Billie," Monica moaned just as she was about to have her orgasm.

Billie's phone began to ring. Monica screamed his name as he moaned hers. Her body started shaking as they came together. Billie looked on the floor at the phone as it continued to ring. It was Nicole. Billie shook his head and tried to reach for it. Monica looked at Billie reaching for the phone and frowned.

This bitch is a pest, she thought as she looked Billie in his eyes and then kissed him.

"This is my time, Daddy," Monica said, then gently grabbed his hand.

Billie sighed as Monica began sucking his dick again. On the ninth ring, the phone went to voice mail. Within seconds, the phone started ringing again. Billie and Monica were now in the sixty-nine position, answering the phone was now the furthest thing from his mind, it again went to voice mail on the ninth ring. Monica smiled to herself. Now Billie would soon be all hers.

* * *

Nicole couldn't shake the feeling that something wasn't right in the tone of Billie's voice when they had spoken. Nicole had to hang up with Billie when the doctor came out to let her know what was going on with her best friend, but right after the doctor had finished telling her the results, Nicole had call Billie right back and his phone went to voice mail. She was sure, but she thought she had heard moaning in the background as they were talking and when they were hanging up. Nicole could have sworn he moaned. Nicole re-dialed his phone number as she walked to Tasha's room. Once again, for the third time it went to voice mail. Nicole stuck the phone in her pocket. "Yeah, maybe I'm assuming things, letting the devil play with my head." Nicole said a quick prayer as she walked into Tasha's room asking that God take away any doubt and unclean thoughts out of her heart and mind.

Nicole walked to the side of Tasha's bed, grabbing her hand, smiling from ear-to-ear. "So bitch," Nicole said, now rubbing Tasha's stomach with her other hand. "The doctor tells me I'm about to be an auntie."

Tasha smiled. "Yeah that's what he's saying. A bitch about to be a mom, Cola! Damn, I'm still shocked," Tasha said, smiling.

"Yeah, we got a lot of shit together, my niece or nephew; but before I go Osh Kosh B'Gosh crazy, I wanna know who the fuck is yo baby's daddy, cause yo ass been keeping secrets, Bitch!"

Tasha opened her mouth to respond just as the nurse came in with her discharge papers.

"Well, Ms. Ward, the doctor said you can go home and also for you to get a lot of rest."

Tasha took the papers, thankful the nurse walked in when she did.

"Thank you, Nurse Kelly."

"You're welcome, sweetie, and don't forget to check up with your OB/GYN when you get back home."

"I won't," Tasha said, not putting her clothes back on as nurse Kelly left the room.

"Okay, bitch, now back to my question," Nicole said, still smiling. "Who is this nigga that got my sister keeping him a secret from me?"

Tasha exhaled and then sighed. "Cola, not now," Tasha said, while putting on her shoes. "I want to see how he feels about this before I go putting him out there and all that" Tasha said, not making eye contact with Nicole, feeling ashamed of herself.

"Who is this motherfucker, the Pope or something? Bitch, fuck what he feels, we keeping it no matter what he wants. You don't need his punk ass, you got me! But okay, Tee, when you ready. You know I'm here. I love you and know that I'll be yo baby's, daddy. Fuck a nigga!"

Tasha laughed then grabbed her discharge papers off the bed as they walked out of the door. "Bitch, if you only knew," Tasha said, while in her mind wondering how she was going to tell Billie she was pregnant with his child. Keeping from Nicole whom the father was and letting him know that aborting her first child was not an option. A tear fell from Tasha's eye as they stepped in the elevator heading back to Los Angeles.

"Even if I did know," Nicole said, pushing the button so the elevator would go down to the parking garage, "I don't give a fuck. You are my sister and I got your back regardless."

Tasha looked in her best friend's eyes. "Bitch, I want you to remember you said that," Tasha said, as the elevator door opened and they got off.

"Oh trust me, I will," Nicole said, smiling. "Bitch, on my life we in this together. Me, you, and Billie will raise this baby if the nigga act shady," Nicole said, then opened the car door.

Tasha got in the car feeling more confused than she had in her whole life. Her last thought before she fell asleep as they rode to the hotel to get their things was that Billie was going to want her to kill her baby.

CHAPTER 23

FOR THE PAST TWO WEEKS, NICOLE had been noticing changes in her body and in her moods. As she stood in the mirror naked about to get dressed for work, Nicole ran her hand over her breasts; they seemed firmer than before and also more fuller. Nicole also had realized that she was having a hard time fitting a few of her bras. *I must be gaining weight*, she thought, as she opened her closet and decided to wear a pink DKNY sweat suit with her pink and white Air Force Ones. Nicole closed the closet and grabbed a pair of thong panties out her drawer. She decided not to wear a bra under her cocaine white wife-beater that she was wearing with her DKNY sweat suit, because her nipples had been sensitive lately and was now always hard. As Nicole put on her thong, she noticed her hips were even fuller and her ass seemed a litter rounder. "Either my under clothes are shrinking or I'm gaining weight," Nicole said, spinning around in the mirror. She put on the sweat suit and completely filled it out. She giggled, loving how her pants fit her now.

"Yeah, a bitch done got thicker."

Nicole put on her shoes, then sat on the bed to tie them up and began thinking about how moody she'd been lately, especially toward Billie. For the last few weeks, anything he would do or didn't do would seem to either piss her off or make her break down and cry. Just like yesterday when he didn't answer his phone on her lunch break and she cried for a thirty minutes feeling hurt for no reason. When Billie called her back, which was before her break was over and explained he was in a meeting with some contractors, Nicole had went off, then cried, saying sorry and told him she need to see him.

Billie told Nicole he would stop by her office as soon as he could and that he loved her, which made her feel a little bit better.

When Billie hung up, he was confused as to why Nicole had wigged out on him, assuming it was because of the shit he was keeping in the closet. Billie went straight to FTD Florist; brought three dozen long-stemmed roses, two boxes of See's candy, one fifteen-inch light brown Teddy Bear and an eight-inch coffee brown Teddy Bear before leaving the flower shop. He picked out three balloons, each one with a different note on it: I love you; I need you; you are very special to me. When he got to her job with his handful of roses, balloons, candy and two teddy bears, all the women's panties in Nicole's office got wet and was smiling as he passed by them saying, "How sweet," "That's so nice," etc. What took the cake was when he stopped at Tasha's office and handed her a single rose, a box of See's candy, and an eight-inch teddy bear, then walked out leaving Tasha speechless. As Billie walked into Nicole's office, one of her female co-worker's said, "Now, that's a real man right there!"

Nicole stood up seeing Billie trying to open her office door, hands full of flowers and balloons. Nicole ran to the door and opened it, smiling from ear to ear, helping him by grabbing the candy, teddy bear and balloons from him.

"Aww, Daddy," she said, closing the door behind him, and then hugging him. "Thank you!"

"You're welcome, Cola. I just wanted to cheer you up. I'm sorry I missed your call. I didn't do it intentionally; my phone was on vibrate in my coat pocket on the back of my chair. I was in a meeting.

"That's okay, Daddy," Nicole said, closing the blinds to her office door, and walking back over to him. She wrapped her arms around his neck. "I don't know what's been coming over me lately; I been really trippin'."

Billie wrapped his arms around her waist as they looked in each other's eyes. He noticed Nicole's nipples standing out through her clothes. *Damn*, he thought as he ran his hand over her soft ass, which caused her to pull closer to him. "I love you, Cola!"

"Hmmm, Daddy, I love you, too." Nicole was horny and wet; she didn't understand what was going on with her body, but right now she wanted some dick. "So now I guess I need to show you I'm sorry for overacting," Nicole said, seductively, and then kissed his lips.

"Baby, you don't have to do anything. I could have texted you or something," Billie said, his conscious getting the best of him.

"No, Daddy, that was all me and I want to show you I'm sorry," Nicole said. She took off her DKNY sweat suit jacket; her nipples could be seen through the shirt.

Billie licked his lips.

Nicole smiled. "I got a treat for you." She bent down in front of him and unzipped his pants. She reached inside, pulling his dick out and began giving him head. Billie moaned as Nicole sucked his dick while stroking him at the same time.

"Fuck, Cola," he moaned as she ran her tongue around the head of his dick.

While still stroking him, she put his dick back in her mouth and went back to bobbing her head, feeling his dick completely hard. Nicole stood up, pulled her sweat pants and thong down around her knees. She bent over her desk and looked over her shoulder. "Come handle yo business, Daddy," Nicole said, then bit her bottom hip.

Billie noticed her ass and hips seemed fuller and that made his dick throb as he came up behind her. Nicole's pussy was dripping wet and Billie could feel the heat come from it as he inserted his dick inside her. Nicole moaned loud as Billie took a deep breath, feeling the walls of her pussy tightly taking a hold of his dick.

"Damn, Cola," Billie moaned as he began going in and out of Nicole, holding on to her waist as she worked her hip and ass in a circular motion.

"Oooh, Daddy," Nicole moaned as Billie took one of his hands off her hips and reached around grabbing one of her breast, massaging her nipples between his fingers.

Nicole, loving the feel of his dick, arched her back letting out a loud moan of pleasure. Nicole began throwing her ass and pussy at Billie, which made him speed up.

"Ooh, Daddy, fuck me," Nicole moaned, feeling her orgasm coming on. "Nigga, hit this pussy, it's yours. Ooooh, Daddy, it's yours."

Billie, now pumping hard in and out of Nicole, was moaning her name. You could hear his thighs slapping against her ass as he went in and out of her.

"Oooh, Daddy, I'm about to cum. Shit, nigga, you gonna make me, oooooooooh ggoood," Nicole yelled as her knees went weak and she began to shake.

Billie, feeling her walls tightened even more, called her name as he too released his load inside her. Still breathing hard, they began adjusting their clothes.

Nicole turned around to face him as he zipped up his pants. She kissed him. "Daddy, I love you."

Billie kissed her back. "I love you, too," he said, then looked down at the front of his jeans. Around the zipper was a big white stain.

They started laughing.

"Damn, Cola, you was really into that, huh?" Billie said, seeing how much she had come.

Nicole giggled. "Fuck you, Daddy. But yeah, I was and it was good, too."

Billie pulled his shirt out of his pants, covering the stain. "Well, I guess I gotta get home so I can change."

Nicole smiled. "How about just to home and get naked? I'll be off work in an hour and we can finish this up."

Billie kissed her and headed for the door. "I'll do that." He winked. "Don't be late."

Nicole put on her jacket, her pussy still throbbing from Billie's beating. "Ooh, believe you me, Daddy, I won't."

Billie walked out Nicole's office, shutting the door behind him. Every woman there was smiling at him as he left.

Tasha sat at her desk holding the flower, candy and teddy bear Billie had handed her then walked out her office. She was so shocked to receive the items that she didn't say thank you. Tasha rubbed her stomach as she thought about the baby that she would soon be bringing into this world. Billie's baby.

Tasha smelled the rose. *He has to really love me to stop by my office first and give me a gift before giving one to Nicole,* she thought, and then noticed the card taped to the box of candy. Tasha smiled and opened the little card.

Dear Tee,

I know this isn't much, but I couldn't just bring Nicole something and not think about you. You have and always will be special to me. I love you and hope you enjoy your gifts.

Love Always, Billie

P.S. You still make me sick with your stankin' ass. Smile

A tear fell from Tasha's eye as she folded the card back up then placed it in her Coach purse. Just as she was about to eat one of her See's candies, her co-worker, Brittany, came busting in her office without knocking.

"Girl, that nigga Nicole got is fine as hell, and I see he is also a sweetheart, too," Brittany said, smiling while taking a seat on Tasha's desk, as she helped herself to one of Tasha's candies. "Shit, I wish a nigga would bring me some flowers," Brittany stated, while chewing on a walnut cluster. "Let alone two or three dozens of roses. The whole office would know how special he made me feel, because they'd hear me telling him while he fucked the shit out of me in my office."

Tasha laughed. "Bitch, you can get the hell out of my office."

Brittany giggled as she hopped off Tasha desk. "Girl, fo' real. I swear on my life, but on the real, I gotta give yo boy his props, because he even dropped you a token of love, just because you're her best friend and it's rare to find a man that's thoughtful like that!"

Tasha nodded her head in agreement. "Bre, I've known that nigga since the fifth grade or sixth grade, he has always been that way," Tasha said, remembering how Billie would always remember her birthday and give her a gift.

"Well, bitch, you a better woman than me, because if I knew that nigga back in grade school and he was laced way back then on how to treat a lady, there is no way I wouldn't kept him for myself. I would have had his ass pussy wiped by homeroom.

Tasha laughed, thinking to herself on how she regretted letting him slip away.

Brittany headed toward the door, turned around, and looked Tasha in her eyes. "Tell yo girl she better keep her gate locked and her dog chained up," Brittany said, with a devilish grin. "Because I'm like Salt and Pepper, I'll take yo man!"

Tasha and Brittany shared a laugh, but Brittany cut it short. "Bitch, I'm serious, good men are hard to find!"

Tasha stood up. "Get your young ass out my office," she stated, pushing Brittany out the door laughing. But in her mind, she was trying to figure out why she didn't keep him to herself.

As Tasha locked her office door, she watched Billie walk by heading for the elevator. Her pussy got wet when he looked at her and winked.

*   *   *

Nicole wasn't feeling too good when she woke up Saturday morning. She and Tasha had been shopping at Babies R Us when she started feeling dizzy. As one of the store employees helped them put the items they purchased in Tasha's car, Nicole passed out. The store employee, whose nametag read Mark, dropped the car seat, which he was putting in the trunk and caught Nicole before she hit the ground. Tasha went into complete hysteria.

"Oh my God, Nicole! Baby...Cola...oh Jesus!"

Mark sat on the ground holding her head up on his lap.

"Call 911," Mark told Tasha as other people began to gather around to see what the commotion was. Five minutes later the ambulance arrived and took Nicole to Kaiser in Bellflower as Tasha followed in her Lexus. Tasha called Billie letting him know what had happed and he was at the hospital as they pulled up.

Billie met them at the emergency room doors as they wheeled Nicole out the ambulance bringing her into the hospital.

"I'm her fiancé," Billie told the medic as they asked him who he was and his relation to the patient. They asked Billie to go to the front desk so he could check her in as they rolled her into a room.

Tasha rushed through the emergency room doors and up the hallway. She was now standing next to Billie, worry written all over her face.

"We was shopping and she…she just passed out."

Billie grabbed her hand. "It's okay, Tee." He hugged her as she began to cry. "Come on, Tee, don't cry please. It's going to be okay," Billie said, trying his best to comfort Tasha.

Tasha held on to Billie tightly as she cried. His scent was driving her insane. She stopped crying held on to him, as she felt safe in his arms.

The nurse came out the room and walked up to Tasha and Billie.

"Hi, I'm Nurse Mitchell, are you two here for Nicole White?"

They broke their embrace. "Yes we are."

"Well so you know she is fine. Just a heat stroke. She hadn't eaten breakfast nor drunk any water all day. It's 98.9 degrees outside, that's a no-no in this kind of heat. She will be okay; we are giving her an IV. She'll be ready to go home shortly."

"Can we go in and see her," Tasha asked, now holding Billie's hand.

"Well she is resting; she will be ready to leave after the IV. I say give her an hour then go in. She is still kind of out of it."

Billie thanked the nurse and asked her to let Nicole know that they would be back in forty-five minutes. Billie and Tasha headed to the cafeteria for a snack while they let Nicole get some rest.

Nicole had told her nurse to lie to Billie and Tasha. She had to get her thoughts together before seeing either of them and wanted to make sure what they had just informed her was true and correct. "I'm pregnant," she said in amazement.. Nicole couldn't believe the news when she was told and if it was really true. She wanted to surprise both Tasha and Billie with the news.

Billie and Tasha stepped into the cafeteria, and it was completely empty, not a visible sign of anyone. Tasha located a sign over the door that read:

Cafeteria hours

6:00 PM to 5:00 PM

8:00 PM to 3:00 AM

Monday thru Friday

Saturdays

From 8:00 AM to 6:00 PM

Sunday

10:00 AM to 3:30 PM

It was 4:45 on Sunday and they had missed it by a little more than an hour.

"Well I guess we could go to the vending machines around the corner," Billie suggested, mad because he really wanted a breakfast burrito.

"Or, you could break me off a little of that dick before we gotta go back up and get Nicole," Tasha said, then pulled her pants and panties down bending over making her ass clap.

Billie's dick was now harder than a steel pole.

"Yo ass is freaky, Tee," Billie stated, watching her ass cheeks clap together like two hands. She completely bent over at the waist and grabbed onto a table, her pussy now seemed to be calling his name.

Tasha looked over her shoulder. "I thought you was hungry," she said, seductively. "Come get your dinner, Daddy."

Billie undid his belt, pulled his pants down to his knees and entered Tasha, thinking about Monica as he stuck all ten inches of his dick inside as she rocked back and forward, as the table slid a few feet with every thrust Billie gave her. Billie's breathing heavily continued hammering away as Tasha moaned his name.

Just as they both were about to cum, they heard footsteps. Billie quickly pulled his dick out of its tightly fitted cave and pulled his pants up as Tasha moaned then sucked her teeth; pissed that she was interrupted. The footsteps got closer as Tasha took her time pulling her pants up with an attitude. Billie laughed as she looked at him and rolled her eyes.

"We could have finished," she said, as her pussy throbbed and tingled.

Just as Billie was about to reply to her, the cafeteria doors opened and Nicole walked in with a look on her face that scared both Billie and Tasha.

Once Nicole was done with her IV, she was told by her nurse that Billie and Tasha had gone to the cafeteria to get something to eat. She decided to meet them down there since she too was a little hungry. As she got to the elevator, she heard moaning and she thought she heard Billie's name being called out. She began walking, following the arrows that pointed toward the location of the cafeteria and the moaning got louder. Her heels clicked off the floor as she picked up her pace.

"Nigga, fuck this pussy," Nicole heard, as she hit the corner now only a few yards away from the cafeteria. When the moaning suddenly stopped, Nicole got to the cafeteria doors and shoved them open to see Billie and Tasha standing there looking at her as she stared at them both wondering why they looked so damn guilty.

Tasha was the first to break the uncomfortable silence as she walked up to Nicole, hugging her. "Bitch, I'm glad you okay," Tasha stated then let Nicole go and looked her over. "Don't ever do me like that again. I almost lost my mind," Tasha said, then smiled.

Nicole was still looking at them strangely, as Billie walked up and kissed her on the lips, hugging her close. "You had me worried, Cola," Billie said, as he held her.

Nicole wrapped her arms around his neck. "Did y'all hear someone moaning about three or four minutes ago," Nicole asked, looking into Billie's eyes.

Billie broke their eye contact, and then looked over at Tasha.

"I didn't hear anything, did you, Tee?"

Tasha shook her head. "Naw Cola, I didn't either."

All the while Tasha was thinking how glad she was that Billie had stopped them when he did. Nicole was still looking into Billie's eyes trying to read him and then kissed him softly on the lips.

"Because, I thought I heard someone getting their fuck on and from what I could hear, the bitch was loving it. Anyhow, I thought I heard your name being called. I was about to go postal in this bitch, then when I opened the door, I see you two. They all shared a laugh. They headed out the cafeteria.

"You know damn well I wouldn't let that go down as long as I'm with him," Tasha said, no longer feeling guilty for fucking with Billie, because he was soon to be her child's father and now could lie with a straight face.

Billie shook his head with a grin. "Is that how you feel, Cola?" Billie asked, looking at her as they got on the elevator, now feeling bad for accusing them.

Nicole smiled. "Y'all should know," she said, smiling at both of them. "That I trust both of you. I'm still on one from passing out. Y'all the last two people I'd think would betray me!"

Nicole pushed the button to go up to the first level, as Billie and Tasha made eye contact then dropped their heads, feeling fucked up for betraying Nicole's trust.

CHAPTER 24

TASHA AND BILLIE HAD MET UP at her house at 9:30 AM. Tasha's calendar was clear and she didn't have any appointments scheduled. She texted Billie and told him to stop by so they could talk. Tasha was now going on a month of being pregnant and not only needed but also wanted to know what Billie was going to do.

As they lay in bed, Tasha kissed him on the chest.

"Daddy, there's something I need to tell you," Tasha said, as Billie ran his finger through her hair. She was unsure of how to come out with what she had to say and how he was going to take it.

"Tee, what is it?" Billie asked, sounding tired and sleepy.

Tasha took a deep breath then exhaled. "Well first off, I want you to know that I love you and always have loved you from the day we sat next to each other in Mrs. Franpatrick's class in the sixth grade and after I tell you this, no matter how you react, I'm still going to love you. You will always have a special place in my heart, no matter what you decide to do!"

Billie giggled. "Oh I've heard this speech a million times, what's next, it's not you it's me and it's over?"

Tasha laughed. "Naw it's not even that, but you might feel that way after I say this. I hope you don't!" Tasha bit her bottom lip as she made eye contact with Billie. "Baby, I'm pregnant!"

Billie damn near bit his tongue off. "You're what?" he exclaimed, now sitting up in bed.

"I'm pregnant. I found out when me and Nicole was in Palm Springs."

Billie got out of bed and started pacing, naked, which made Tasha nervous.

Billie looked at Tasha. "Is it mine, Tee, or are you fucking someone else, too?"

"Nigga, fuck naw. I'm not fucking nobody else and fuck you, I'm not no ho, Billie. You the only nigga fucking me." A tear fell from Tasha's eye; she was more than hurt that he would even ask her some shit like that.

"Tee, I'm sorry," Billie said, trying to wrap his arms around her.

Tasha snatched away from him. "Nigga, don't touch me," she yelled, moving to the other end of the bed.

"Tee, I didn't mean to offend you, but I just assumed you had someone. I mean damn, you beautiful; Tee, you're a good woman. I didn't mean for you to take it like that, because I don't even, nor have I ever thought of you as a ho. I deeply care about you, always have and I love you, too!"

Billie now all shook up by the news began pacing again.

Tasha grabbed a pillow and held it close to her chest. "So what are we going to do?" she asked, watching him pace.

Billie's mind was racing. Monica was pregnant and she was keeping their baby; he was even thinking about leaving Nicole after Monica had the baby, so he could be a daddy to his child.

"Damn, Tee," Billie said, as he burned a whole in her carpet. "I know you want to keep it, huh?" Billie looked in her eyes as he waited for her answer.

"Yeah, I'm keeping my baby," Tasha said, with an attitude. "I don't believe in abortions and if I did, I wouldn't kill my first child."

Billie sighed. "Tee you're Nicole's best friend, how are we going to tell her this? We gotta tell her it can't be hidden, because sooner or later she is going to notice that the baby look like me or has my eyes or nose, or shit...something. Since you want to keep the baby, tell me how we gonna do this. Please tell me, Tee!"

"Nigga, I don't give a fuck about none of that," Tasha said, now getting to her feet knocking her phone off the dresser as she stood up making eye contact with Billie.

"I don't give a fuck what you tell her or what she thinks at this point. I'm not going to kill my baby so she can be happy. I already gave her you like a fool. I love Nicole with all my heart, but my child is not an option. So you need to figure out something, because I'm keeping my baby. How you handle this is up to you, but know this, I will not act like my child does not have a father so think hard and fast. I don't want to hurt Cola, but I'm not going to hurt our child!"

Billie took a deep breath. "Fuck, Tee, what do you want or expect for me to do?" He ran his hands over his head and resumed pacing the floor.

"That's just it, I don't know right now. I'm just as confused as you are. We have a baby on the way so we need to come up with a plan because as long as you play the part of a father in our child's life, I'll be happy, if that means telling Nicole about us, then so be it. Trust me she will get over it, she will have to. She doesn't have a choice!"

Billie laid back down in the bed trying to figure out just what would be his best move, as Tasha looked at him angrily waiting to hear what he had decided.

*   *   *

Nicole decided today would be the day she would tell Billie and Tasha she was pregnant. Nicole knew Billie was leaving for Cancun later on this evening and planned to tell him before he left. She wanted to give him something to think about while he was away from home as well as a reason for him to hurry back. Nicole smiled, thinking of how happy he would be that their dream of having a baby together had finally come true. Nicole would be happy no matter what sex the baby would be, but she was hoping for a boy, because she knew that's what Billie wanted. Whenever she and Billie would snuggle up in bed and talk, Billie would always say, "If we ever are blessed to have a baby, I hope we have our son first that way he can protect his sister."

Nicole rubbed her stomach and smiled. "Your daddy is going to be overjoyed about you coming into this world. He might even cancel that trip to Cancun," Nicole said, as she got up from her desk and walked over to her window, looking out at a beautiful view of the City of Lakewood. Nicole had already talked to her boss so that she didn't have to come back to work after lunch. She and Billie had already said their goodbyes this morning, so he was going to be totally surprised when she popped up before he left and told him the good news. Tasha was in the field, during their lunch break today where they meet up. Nicole was going to tell her best friend that they would be bringing their first child into the world around the same time. Nicole was so happy that she and Tasha could share this moment together. Today was Tasha's day to pick the place for lunch, so she picked a spot in San Pedro called Pro-Ta-Calls. It had bomb ass food and Nicole couldn't wait to get her eat on. It was 11:15 AM, and Nicole needed to start on her way.

Nicole started getting her things together to leave; she shut down her computer, grabbed her purse and walked out her office shutting her door. She headed to the elevator with a Kool-Aid smile on her face. Her phone rung as she was getting on it. She looked at the caller ID. It was Tasha. She pressed answer then put the phone to her ear.

"Bitch, where you at?" Nicole said into the phone as the elevator doors closed.

Tasha was still sitting on the bed waiting for Billie's answer. She hadn't noticed that she had knocked her phone off the dresser, nor did she realize it had called Nicole when it hit the floor.

"So what the fuck you going to do?" Tasha asked as Billie sat back up getting out of bed again.

Billie had made his decision in his mind. He knew just what he had to do. He looked at Tasha, and then started pacing again. "Look Tee, in a few months we can tell Nicole I'm the father of your baby, if that's what you want. I don't know how she is going to take it, but it is what it is."

Tasha rolled her eyes. "We don't have to do all that. I just need to know you're going to be around for me and your child!"

Billie looked at Tasha with a smirk on his face. "I'm always around, ain't I? I'm here now, ain't I?"

"You know what the fuck I mean, nigga. It's a baby involved now, someone that's going to need your guidance and love."

Billie nodded his head. "Yeah, we will figure out something," Billie said, while getting dressed. "We will talk about this more when I come back from Cancun."

Tasha rolled her eyes as she lay back in bed. "Yeah, you can count on that and you better call me while your ass is out there," Tasha said, as Billie grabbed his keys then walked out the bedroom door.

"Yeah, I got you!" Tasha heard him say as she jumped out the bed and went into the bathroom slamming the door.

Billie got into his Jag, and then placed his head on the steering wheel. As he sat there lost in thought, he realized he had become just like the men that he never wanted to be like. He was doing Nicole just as those men had done his mother and was having two kids by two different women. Billie was just like his dad. He drove out of Tasha's driveway, hating himself for what he had let happen to his life for some pussy.

***

Nicole held the phone to her ear listening closely as the elevator went down to the first floor. She could hear Tasha arguing with someone, but couldn't figure out or put her finger on who that someone was. Once at the first floor, Nicole ran out her office building and headed to her car. She was trying to hear a location or a hint of any kind of where Tasha was at so she could go help her. Nicole knew that in the field, sometimes families could get crazy when fucking with their kids.

Just as Nicole was getting in her car, she heard the voice of the person Tasha was arguing with clear as day. It was Billie.

What the fuck they arguing about? Nicole asked herself, as she got in her Jag and her phone paired with the cars blue tooth system. Nicole could now hear everything crystal clear. Tears ran down her face as she listened to her best friend's conversation with her fiancé. Nicole got more than an earful. She continued to listen until she couldn't take it anymore. Nicole pushed end on her phone then drove out the parking lot of her job. The tears flowed down her face freely as she got on the 105 Freeway. Thirty minutes later, she found herself at Hertz Rent-a-Car. An hour and a half after that, she was sitting across the street from her and Billie's house in one of their neighbor's driveway.

"These motherfuckers got me fucked up," she said to herself as she sent Tasha to voice mail for the twenty-sixth time. "How could they do me like this?" Nicole watched her front door and garage from across the street. Tears ran down her face as she began rubbing her stomach. She closed her eyes and took a deep breath. "I can't believe they did me like this!"

CHAPTER 25

MONICA WAS ON THE OTHER END of the phone when she heard Nicole clock the gun and began questioning Billie. She heard Nicole when she told him to hand her the phone. Monica was smart enough to know not to let Nicole know it was she on the other end of the phone, but she wasn't going to let Billie get hurt either. Monica loved him and was in love with him. When Nicole took the phone and started yelling into it, Monica played her position to a tee, she even changed her voice and got Nicole to say who she was, so if it was necessary, Monica could identify the bitch.

"Fuck," Monica yelled, as the line was disconnected and she was left holding the phone. Monica was at the office, waiting for Billie to go home, pack his bags, and then come get her so they could go to the airport and leave for Cancun.

"I can't let this bitch hurt my baby," Monica said out loud, as she grabbed the glock Billie kept in the desk for the office. She decided to go to his house and make sure he was okay. From what Monica heard, Nicole had a gun and Monica wasn't going to lose Billie. Monica swore she wouldn't be another single black woman, raising a child on her own.

Monica locked up the office, and then hopped in her BMW x5. She headed up La Cienega going eighty-five miles per hour. Three minutes later, she was pulling in Billie's driveway, parking behind his Jag. Monica could hear yelling as she got out the car, and then she heard three shots.

"Aw hell naw," Monica stated as she ran to the door. It wasn't closed completely, because the doormat was jamming it. Monica slowly pushed the door open a little. She heard the conversation Nicole was having over the phone with whom Monica figured was 911, because Nicole was asking for help and saying Billie was shot.

Monica pushed the door a little more with her gun at her side, trying to see if she could see Billie as she looked around. She noticed him on the floor with Nicole standing over him.

Ooh, hell naw, bitch, Monica thought, as she raised the gun, sliding into the house through the front door as Nicole was yelling at Billie asking him about a baby.

"How the fuck does she know?" Monica asked herself, as she saw Nicole raise the gun to Billie's head.

"Are you going to make her abort it or do you want her to keep it?"

Billie looked away. "I...I..." he stammered.

Pop, pop, pop!

"Bitch, I'm keeping it," Monica said, firing three rounds at Nicole as she tried to turn around to see the face of the voice she heard.

Nicole caught one of Monica's bullets in her back, one in her shoulder and the third one missed her as she tripped over Billie, dropping her gun.

Billie looked up to see Monica standing over Nicole, hitting her over the head with the butt of the 9mm.

"Bitch, you talk too much that's why you got caught slipping," Monica said, picking up Nicole's gun then spitting in her face.

Billie looked in Monica's eyes in shock.

"It's okay, baby I'm here," Monica said, as she sat down next to him, looking him over to make sure he was not badly hurt.

Billie looked over at Nicole then back at Monica. "How did you know?"

"Shhhh, babe, rest okay? I knew and I'm here," Monica said, cutting him off as she rubbed his head.

Billie laid his head on her lap. He could hear the sirens coming. "Go put those guns up now," he ordered as he thought about the police.

Monica jumped up, ran out the front door to her car and placed both guns under her seat then ran back into the house. Nicole gave a little moan and tried to open her eyes.

Monica grabbed her hair and banged her head on the floor. "Naw, bitch, you stay sleep!" Monica began rubbing Billie's head again just as the cops ran into the house with their guns drawn.

"Let me do the talking," Billie said, as the cops looked at them, and then asked if the suspect was still in the house.

"No," Billie answered, "they're gone."

Hearing this, the cops put their guns away, and then radioed in for an ambulance.

Monica kept Billie's head in her lap. "I love you, Billie," Monica said, as the cop checked Nicole's pulse.

"She has a pulse, Sergeant," the white officer stated as the Sergeant radioed for an ambulance for the second time.

Monica kissed Billie on the forehead as two Techs came running in and began taking Billie's vital signs. They hooked him up to an IV.

Billie took a deep breath, and then exhaled. "I love you too, Mo, and thank you for saving my life!"

Monica smiled as they put him on a gurney. "I just didn't save your life," Monica said, holding his hand as they rolled him to the ambulance, "I saved our future."

Monica hopped in the ambulance with Billie, never letting his hand go.

EPILOGUE

NICOLE LAY IN HER HOSPITAL BED, wondering how she got caught slipping while handling her business. She could only remember hearing, "Bitch I'm keeping it!" Next, she felt a hot fire running through her before being knocked out. "Who the fuck was that?" Nicole kept asking herself, playing the scene and woman's voice over and over in her head. The doctor's had told her she was very lucky and also that she hadn't lost her baby, but had two bullet wounds that would heal in time and that neither one was fatal.

Who the fuck shot me? she wondered, wracking her brain, still not able to place the voice. Her nurse came in bringing her lunch.

"Excuse me, do you know if a Billie Ward is checked in this hospital? He is my fiancé. I think we came here together."

The lady gave Nicole a loving smile. "He was discharged earlier this morning, sweetie," the nurse said, walking out the door. "Well, I thought his wife took him home, but if you're his fiancé, I guess she was a good friend."

Nicole's mouth got dry as she lost her voice for a second in shock. "Wait," she yelled, as the nurse was about to turn the corner.

"Yes, sweetie," the nurse said, stopping and facing Nicole. She took a few steps back in the room.

"I'm sorry I yelled, but do you remember the woman's name he left with?" Nicole asked, now sitting up in her bed.

"Hmmm, let me see. Don't quote me on this, but if I'm not mistaken, I think her name was Monica. Yeah, it was Monica!"

Nicole slammed back in her bed. "Thank you!"

"No problem," the nurse said, now leaving.

As the nurse turned the corner, Nicole began crying as she remembered the last words she heard before she was shot and she could now place the voice.

"Naw, bitch, I'm keeping it." She didn't want to believe it, but she knew it was true.

"Ooh, my God," Nicole said, now crying uncontrollably. "Monica is pregnant, too!"

Nicole began rubbing her stomach as she cried herself to sleep with a deep hatred in her heart and revenge on her mind.

Billie with his wife, Athena Shell

ABOUT THE AUTHOR

Billie Dureyea Shell was born in Compton, California. He graduated from California State University of Northridge with a BA degree in Business Administration. Billie has five children. He is an entrepreneur, he loves reading, writing and playing music. His hobbies are writing and bowling.

Billie plans to write at least two books per year. Billie states, "I want to leave a literary legacy."